Fifty Fragments of the Inner Self

Amrita Pritam

HIND POCKET BOOKS
An imprint of Penguin Random House

HIND POCKET BOOKS

USA | Canada | UK | Ireland | Australia
New Zealand | India | South Africa | China | Singapore

Hind Pocket Books is part of the Penguin Random House group of companies whose addresses can be found at www.hindpocketbooks.com

Published by Penguin Random House India Pvt. Ltd
4th Floor, Capital Tower 1, MG Road,
Gurugram 122 002, Haryana, India

Penguin Random House India

First published in Hind Pocket Books 2000
This edition published in Hind Pocket Books by Penguin Random House India 2022

Translation : Tara Meenakshi Sekhri

10 9 8 7 6 5 4 3 2

ISBN 9789353490331

Printed at Manipal Technologies Limited, India

HIND POCKET BOOKS

Fifty Fragments of the Inner Self

Amrita Pritam was an Indian maverick writer and poet. She is considered the first eminent female Punjabi writer, novelist and poet of the 20th century. Her writing is equally loved by the people of India and Pakistan. In her over 6 decades long career, she produced over hundred works, including poetry, essays, novels, biographies, etc. She was honoured with prestigious awards like the 'Sahitya Akademi,' 'Bharatiya Jnanpith,' and 'Padma Vibhushan' among many others. One of her most famous novels titled 'Pinjar' was made into a movie of the same name. She also penned an autobiography, in which she expressed her audacity by writing about her personal life, which might be considered 'controversial' by many, even in contemporary India. Amrita Pritam is most remembered for her poem, 'Ajj aakhaan Waris Shah nu.'

CONTENTS

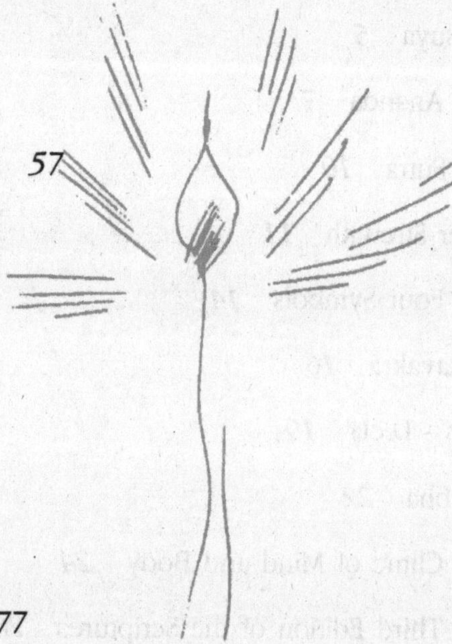

Adi-Leela

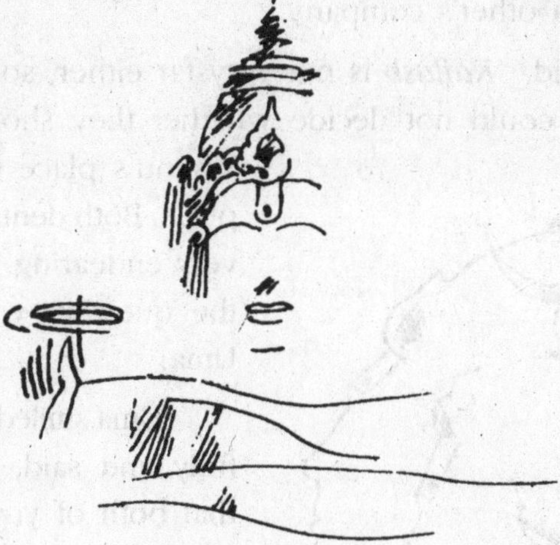

They Say That Once Vishnu was asleep in his divine abode, *Vaikunth*, when he had a dream. He dreamt that Lord Shiva stood before him in a dancing mien — all radiant like the moon and the shimmering stars. When he awoke, he told Lakshmi, "It seems that Shiva is remembering me today. Come, let us go and meet him."

Both of them set out for *Kailash Parvat*. They had hardly gone some distance when they saw Shiva coming towards them. He was accompanied by Uma. When they came closer, Vishnu and Shiva met and embraced each other. They came to know that Shiva also dreamt the previous night.

So he too started from home in order to meet Vishnu who said, "This is only mid-way. Let us go to *Vaikunth* and sit a while in each other's company.

Shiva said, "*Kailash* is not very far either, so let us go there." They could not decide whether they should go to Vishnu's place or Shiva's place. Both demands were very endearing. So finally the question was put to Uma.

Uma smiled meaningfully and said, "It seems that both of you are one spirit, one being. *Vaikunth* itself is *Kailash* and *Kailash* is *Vaikunth*. I am myself Lakshmi and Lakshmi is Uma. So if you agree both of you ought to go to your own respective abodes."

As they began walking, Vishnu felt that he was leaving for *Vaikunth* in the form of Shiva himself and Lord Shiva likewise felt that he was walking towards *Kailash* in the very form of Vishnu.

Prashna Leela

Devi Asked A Question, "O, Lord of gods! Do explain to me the form of this *Kauliki* energy that governs this entire universe and exists in every object and every heart."

Shiva replied, "O, fortunate one, listen to the description of the unanswerable element which is the basis of all answers!

"This expansive sky of my heart in which the *Kauliki* process is present in an eternal shape, is known as *anuttor*, the unanswerable. That is all-pervasive....

"Thus, every question is a *Prashna Leela* of *Devi* — Devi's play of questions. It has rippled fourth from this state of the unanswerable, which includes the answer. This same state of *anuttor* is rudrayamal which comprises of *Rudr* (Shiva) and *Rudra* (*Shakti*).

"The word *Kul* which is used by Devi is the creativity of elements — sky, fire, air, water and earth. She, herself being their *Shakti*, is Kulnayyika, is the heroine of Kul. And the word *Kauliki* used by her is Shiv-element, which is contained in herself."

Devi asks questions in the science, *Bhairav-Tantra*, which appear to be philosophical. But *TANTRA* is a science, it is not philosophy. Therefore when Devi asks, "My lord, what is your truth?" Shiva answers —

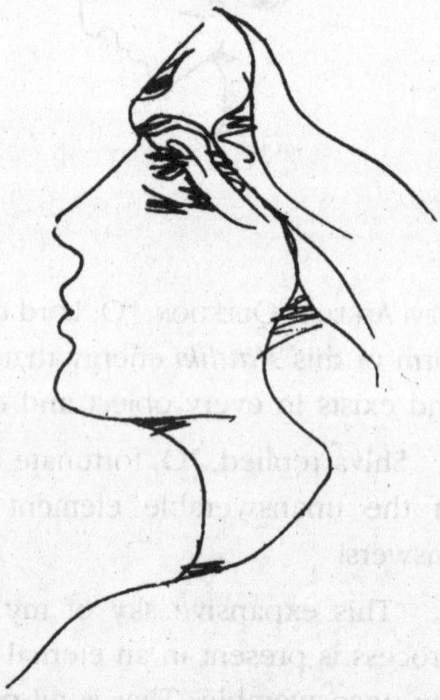

"O, Devi! The experience happens between the two breaths — after inhaling and just before exhaling."

In *tantra*, DOING IS KNOWING. These methods may be known to those alone who have the thirst for knowledge. For them does *Devi* enact this *Prashna Leela*, to lead them to the answers.

Anasuya

It So Happened That Gauri, Lakshmi and Saraswati marvelled at the exalted fame of Anasuya. So they sent Shiva, Vishnu and Brahma to test her. The three gods went disguised as *Sadhus* and asked Anasuya for alms. As she was about to give them alms they said, "Not in this way. Alms will be acceptable, O' Devi, only if you are not clad." Anasuya perceived curiously into this wonder. She turned her mind's eye inwards and meditated for a while. Soon she realized what the secret was. She brought some water from the pitcher, cast a charm on it and sprinkled it on the three of them. Within no time the three gods were transformed into infants.

Anasuya then picked them up, took them inside the hut and started feeding the three small children one by one.

Seeing this, Attri Rishi also smiled that the three gods were being fed on his wife's breast.

All the three devis on the other hand got worried because their husbands had not returned. So they came to the door of Anasuya. She received them respectfully, took them inside the hut and showed them the three infants saying, "Here are your husbands." The devis begged for forgiveness.

Again she took some water out of the pitcher, cast *mantras* and sprinkled it on them. All three came back to their original forms. Begging to be forgiven, they said to her —

"Devi, do ask for any boon." Promptly, Anasuya expressed her innermost wish —

"Be it so! May all three of you take birth from my womb."

And... the legend goes that Anasuya did give birth to three boys. They were Durvasa, Chandrama, and Dattatroya born out of the partial energy of Lord Shiva, Brahma and Vishnu.

Dev Ananda

HISTORY JUST STOOD STILL AND witnessed Dev Ananda of the village Brahmana Kund when she conceived in her womb the twenty fourth *teerthankar*, Mahavir. Never ever had it happened in the tradition of *teerthankars.* Every *teerthankar* is born from the womb of a queen of a *Kshatriya* family.

This event created a slight worry in the abode of gods. It was noted that each *teerthankar's* mother had fourteen dreams of *Airawat*, the elephant, the sun, the moon and heaps of jewels at the time of giving birth. So did Dev Ananda have all those dreams...

It is said that Raja Indra sent a god, Harinegmeshi, to

earth at that time with the purpose of changing the conception of the *teerthankar.* Inducing a sound sleep on Dev Ananda, Harinegmeshi removed the pregnancy of eighty-two days and bestowed it in the womb of Queen Trishala of Kund Gram.

Even Queen Trishala had fourteen dreams and when Mahavir was born in 599 B.C. Raja Indra himself came and offered ***namaskar*** to Queen Trishala. He said, "O, mother with a womb full of jewels, I offer you my salutations." Then taking the infant from the mother's lap, sitting on *Pandu Shila* of *Meru Parvat,* he bathed him with many pitchers of water brought from the skies.

Mahavira lived in the palace of his father, King Siddharta and his mother Trishala for thirty years. When his parents were no more, he clad himself in the robes of a Sadhu. It was the fourteenth year of that period of meditation when Mahavir reached Brahmana Kund, as he went imparting spiritual knowledge to thousands of people. Dev Ananda, along with her husband Rishabhdutt also came for the *darshan* of Mahavira. Rishabhdutt was a scholar of *Vedas.* Therefore, Mahavir sitting calm and tranquil, kept on answering many a question asked by him. When Dev Ananda looked at Mahavir, she just sat like a divine image...

By chance Mahavir's disciple Gandhar Gautam noticed this and threw a questioning glance at Mahavir. Mahavir said, "This is my mother, Gautam, I was in her womb for eighty-two days."

At that moment Dev Ananda enclosed the image of

Mahavir's face within her eyes, which were gradually closing in ecstatic trance. The next event could only be witnessed by the heavenly bodies and not by the people of this earth.

Dev Ananda cast off the old age of so many years like a robe from the body and took up the garb of youthful bloom. Her imagination held her spellbound and with closed eyes she was fondling child Mahavir in her lap. Even the gods offered *Namaskar* to this divine spectacle of motherly affection.

The people of this earth only know that, Dev Ananda and Rishabhdutt sat at Mahavir's feet and received *Deeksha*, the sacred initiation, from him.

Jain-Sutra

THERE IS BUT ONE CREATION in this world which emanated from the ripples of a long silence...

Osho tells us that Mahavir was silent for years. He did not express any Sutra by speech or by writing. But his eleven disciples continued to be by his side all through. They observed and felt Mahavir's silence vibrating. Whatever each of them heard within himself, separately, was all alike. What the eleven disciples heard was identical. They penned down the same. And .... THAT.... is called *Jain Sutra*.

Inner Strength

IT IS SAID THAT ONCE Mahavir and Goshalak were going somewhere. As they were passing through a village, on the way they saw a plant. Goshalak put a question to Mahavir, "What is your opinion? Will this plant ever blossom? Will it last or not till the flowers come?"

Mahavir observed the plant very carefully and stood silent for a while. Then he said, "Yes, this plant shall survive till its bloom."

Goshalak advanced and uprooted the plant even as Mahavir was watching it. Then he laughed, "Now, how can it ever flower?" Mahavir just smiled and said nothing. Both of them proceeded to the village where they were going to. Meanwhile it started raining. There was a heavy downpour, so heavy, that instead of halting for a day as was planned they

had to stay for seven days. After these seven days, on their return they had to take the same route. When they reached that particular spot where the plant was pulled and flung away, they saw that it was standing straight with a big scarlet flower, in full bloom, growing on it.

Now, Goshalak was bewildered as to how this could happen. He asked Mahavir, "I am amazed. I had pulled it from the very root. How has it taken root again? How did you prophesy and declare that plant would flower again?"

Mahavir replied, "The reason why I stood here and observed it closely was to see the possibilities of its inner self, to see the extent of its inner strength. I observed whether it was keen to live or it wished to die. If it had wished to die, it would have died when you helped it to. I knew that you would lead it to the path of death, and I noticed that the plant willed to live, and has returned from the path of death. Due to the rain, some mud got collected around it. With that support it has propped up once again. It has taken root."

This was the plant's strength in its inner-self, its inner-strength.

The Four Symbols

THEY SAY THAT WHEN RAM returned from Lanka, he wished to bring about *Ram Rajya* in Ayodhya. That time Rishi Vashishth was sent for. He said, "In order to bring Ram Rajya, O' Ram, you will first have to transform yourself from Ram to Vishnu. You will have to hold all the four symbols of Vishnu in four hands.

"In one of his hands, Vishnu has a lotus flower. This means blossoming out of inner consciousness. This symbol signifies the conduct of the king who has to bloom out of the inner energy, being totally oblivious of the slush around. Will you be able to do it?"

"The second symbol that Vishnu carries is the *gada*. It is the sign of bravery. It is not the symbol of physical force alone but also of spiritual strength. With the help of its power, the aggressor has to be ousted from your land and, at the same time, you have to eliminate the negative energies like falsehood and oppression from your own people. These dark and negative energies like ego and greed have to be gotten rid of from your own mind too. Will you be able to do so"

"Vishnu has a *chakra*, a bladed discus in his third hand. This wheel is the sign of the speed of Time. This gives new meanings to civilization, the progress of art and the ever novel acquisitions of science...

"Listen, Ram, in his fourth hand Vishnu has a *Shankh*, or conch-shell. The voice of learning, the inner sound of this conch should spread far and wide, it should pervade the entire atmosphere with music so that the subtle elements of the inner soul are awakened. Not of the king alone, O' Ram, but also of the subjects."

Ashtavakra

During The Era Of Raja Janak, Rishi Ashtavakra was born from the womb of Sumati, the daughter of Rishi Udalak. His father was a *Kahod Brahman*. It is said that one day when his father was teaching his students the *Vedas*, he called from the womb itself and pointed out to his father, "This chanting is wrong. There is a mistake." History has it that the father pronounced, "Child, in the womb and by birth you shall have a *vakra*. After you are born, may you have full eight *vakras* on you." They say that this child had eight twists on his body by birth itself. Owing to this, he was given the name 'Ashtavakra.'

Our history is full of symbolism and what has been

stated as outward signs are not in fact external symptoms but are indications of inner experiences.

Experienced persons, Shri Om Prakash Mahajan among them, explain it thus. This was an indication of that Kundalini which was manifest in the eight energy centres of the body. That is why this great scholar used to have discourse with Raja Janak very often. This very dialogue is known as the *'Ashtavakra Gita.'*

From *Mooladhar-chakra* to *Sahasarar* generally seven of them are counted. But many maintain that there are eight. Between *Agyachakra* and *Sahasarar* one more energy point is counted.

The energy arising from *mooladhar* always flows in a serpentine movement. It flows in a crooked way and hence this Rishi is called Ashtavakra (eight twists).

In a similar instance, Deval Rishi was Asit Rishi's son, who used to sit in penance on the mountain Gandhamadan. Once, the *Apsara* Rambha was desirous of mating but the Rishi's mind was unshaken. At this Rambha uttered, "May your handsome frame have eight vakras." Deval Rishi had transformed the sexual energy into the inner energy. Therefore, his mind was not disturbed and what Rambha uttered was not a curse either. It was a salutation to this energy. Deval Rishi is also known as Ashtavakra.

So this was a symbol and not an external symptom. It was the journey of Kundalini which had reached *Brahma*

Randhra and which imparted the Brahm-Gyan. This Brahm-Gyan is the *Mahagita* of Ashtavakra.

The *Gita* of Ashtavakra is not a journey of meditation but is a destination of the ultimate realization where the *namaskar* is for 'Self.'

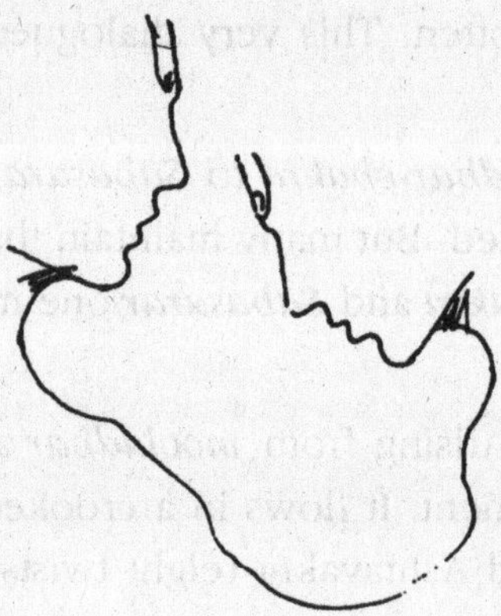

Nath-Leela

THE WORD 'NATH' WAS FIRST connoted to the *yogi* form of Lord Shiva — Adi Nath. From Adinath, the *Deeksha* of the science of *Yoga* was first imparted to Matsyendra Nath, and from him to Gorakhnath. Once Matsyendra Nath said to Gorakhnath, "I want to enter the inner-self. Therefore you keep my gross-body safe and with care. I shall be moving around with the help of my subtle-body."

Many days went by. A vague rumour travelled to Gorakhnath that Matsyendra Nath was living in the royal palace of Sangal Island with pretty princesses, that he was totally immersed in the mood of dancing.

Gorakhnath got extremely worried and was enraged at this degeneration of Nath. He felt that the *yoga* of his master and saint was blemished. Now the Nath-tradition would be heading for a downfall. Gorakhnath started on a long journey in order to save Matsyendra Nath. On the way he met *rasdharis.* He asked them, "Where are you going?", and he came to know that they were going to the court of Matsyendra on the island of Sangal. His brow blazed with anger. But soon taking control of himself he mingled with the group of *rasdharis.*

On the way wherever these devotional dancers played music or sang songs, Gorakhnath too accompanied them on the tabla giving beats.

At last they arrived at the royal court of Sangal Island. Gorakh saw that his Nath was sitting along with many beautiful women on the raised platform. Music and dance performances were going on in front of him. Gorakhnath sat disguised as a *rasdhari* with suppressed anger. When it was the turn of *raśdharis* to sing and play, he gave the beats of the *tabla* with such intensity that the entire court resounded, "Machchander, do wake up. Gorakh has arrived..."

Nath simply smiled. He called Gorakh to him. Gorakh spoke in heated words, "What kind of inner-self is this? What kind of meditation is going on? Get up. Come with me to the *yoga-ashram*."

Nath laughingly replied, "Your arrogance of *Siddhi* has not yet left you!"

As Gorakh turned around, he found that Nath had suddenly vanished. Gorakhnath woke his companions up to search for Nath.

His companions laughed, "Gorakhji, whom are you looking for? Who is lost? Our Nath Matsyendra was engrossed in meditation sitting in the cave of Bhanwar for a very long time."

Noticing his perplexity, the companions told Gorakhnath, "This was *Nath-Leela*. It was meant to break your arrogance of *Siddhi*."

Sulabha

THERE WAS A *BRAHMA-VADINI* by the name of Sulabha during the period of Raja Janak. She had heard of the greatness of Raja Janak and that learned scholars came to his court very frequently. Often scholastic discussions and discourses took place there.

Sulabha changed her appearance of *Sanyasini*, disguised herself as a beautiful woman and went to Raja Janak. Raja gave her immense honour and respect. From her appearance he deduced that she was a learned woman. Hence he opened a discussion on *brahma-gyan* and in the course of it he apprised her of his own state of mind. It was firmly set on inner-knowledge, although he was in the royal palace...

Sulabha summed up the dialogue and said, "O' Revered king, the journey of the soul has not ended yet. In your court the spirit of debate is still maintained and so is your interest in victory and defeat. You still delight in discussions and arguments of debate."

Brahma-Gyan is yet to be attained. After reaching it, there is neither *shastra* nor *shastarth* but only silence.

The Clime of Mind and Body

A HILLOCK STANDS ON THE bank of Rewa in Maheshwar even today. It is here that the religious discussion between Adi Shankaracharya and Mandan Mishra took place. Sharda, who is considered a form of Saraswati, was there to decide the victory and the defeat. Both of them were offered similar asanas to sit. Having plucked fresh flowers, she strung two garlands looking alike with the same kind of flowers. Now, she put them round the necks of these two learned scholars and said, "During the discussion, the garlands will decide the winner and the loser. The wearer of the garland whose flowers fade first will be considered to have lost...."

Sharda maintained that he who possessed intellectual clarity, power of thinking, self-confidence will be calm and peaceful. His voice will be like cool spring. Therefore, the flowers around his neck will breathe the tranquil air of his body. They will remain fresh and blooming for a longer time. On the other hand, one who does not have a clear intellect or a strong sense of logic or whose self-confidence staggers, will have frustration emanating from within him. His voice will become harsh, the circulation of blood rapid in his veins and his breath will become hot. Hence the flowers around his neck will wither sooner."

Adi Shankaracharya could see into the secret of her farsightedness and smiled meaningfully.

Mandan Mishra happily gazed at the garland round his neck.

The flowers full of bloom blossomed even more because here was one who identified their inner-soul that day.

The Third Edition of the Scriptures

A Buddhist Mendicant Took The responsibility of translating and publishing some Buddhist scriptures into Japanese. It took him a long time to collect money from people to meet the requirement of this project. Just as sufficient money was collected and the books were ready to go to the press, a dreadful famine struck the country. People started starving for even a morsel. At that time, this Buddhist Monk purchased foodgrains with the money saved over so many years and distributed among the people.

As the conditions improved, this mendicant trudged

about from city to city, from village to village, once again obtaining funds for publishing these books. After many years when enough money was accumulated, there were such floods in the country that village after village was wiped out. The Buddhist monk gave away all that money in helping the people who were dispossessed of their homes.

By this time, he had reached the age of seventy. Now it took him another twenty years to raise collections of sufficient funds for the publication of these scriptures. He was ninety years old when they finally got published.

History stands witness to what is written on those books --

"This is the third edition of the scriptures. The first two editions have been offered to the sacrificial fire of the great *yagya* for the people. Hence those rare editions are not available now....."

History proves that there was someone who gave this honourable term of sacrificial-ceremony for humanity to this philanthropic work for people in the time of misery. In a *yagya*, the hand that makes the offering is freed from all ego and arrogance.

Lin-Chi

Osho Narrates A Touching And tender conversation about how the mystery of *Para Bindu* submerged in the inner consciousness of the human being, after a long journey.

There was a *dervesh* called Lin-Chi. He worshipped Buddha. While worshipping, he reached a stage that one day he removed Buddha's idol and destroyed it. His friend saw this and he rebuked him, "Have you gone mad, Lin-Chi?" He replied, "Till I thought that I am, I was sure that Buddha also existed. Now since I am not there any more, most certainly Buddha too does not exist."

But that same night his companions saw that he was

praying to Lord Buddha and making his offerings. They were astonished and Lin-Chi explained, “I am offering my thanks to Buddha who is not there. He helped me to attain this state of not being.”

This NOT BEING is transcending oneself ... This is the

secret of worship, that is to go beyond the idol. This is the secret of form that has to become formless, from the visible creation to this originating point...

And from this point to *Para Bindu*, that is, beyond this originating point.

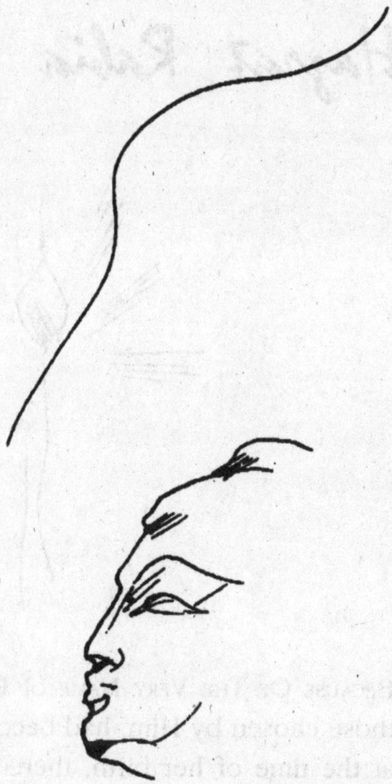

Hazrat Rabia Basri

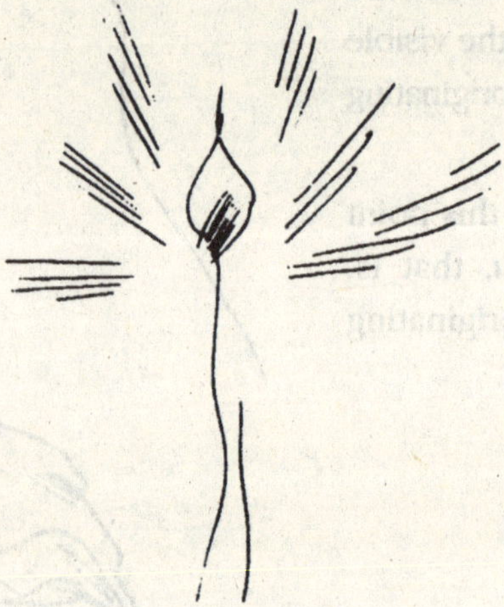

Because Of The Very Name of Rabia, the lovers of God and those chosen by Him, had become gloriously renowned. But at the time of her birth, there wasn't even a drop of oil at home to apply on her navel. There wasn't a piece of cloth to wrap the body of this divine infant. The oil-less lamp looked on from a corner of the house, at the strange ways of God. Rabia's mother told Rabia's father, "Please, go and borrow some oil from the neighbours". But this blessed man only touched the neighbours' doors and returned to say that no one opened the door. The fact was, that, this godly man did not believe in begging from anyone except God.

That night as he slept, he heard an unknown voice. "This daughter of yours is chosen by God; she will attain His grace. Because of her, one thousand religious people who pray to me, will be pardoned." That divine voice also said, "Write my message on a paper and send it to the ruler of Basra. You are accustomed to send salutations and prayers to me hundred times daily, on Friday you do the same four hundred times. But last evening you forgot to do so.

As an atonement to that, you give four hundred dinars to the man who has sent this note for you."

When he woke up from this dream, Rabia's father wept bitterly. But as he had been commanded, he wrote down his full dream on a paper and sent it to the ruler of Basra. As soon as he read the note, the ruler of Basra sent four hundred dinars to Rabia's father. He also distributed ten thousand dirhams amongst the needy and the fakirs. He was grateful to God that He remembered him.

Conditions changed with time. There was a famine in Basra. By that time Rabia's parents were no more. Her three elder sisters disappeared, no one knew where to earn their bread. Now, Rabia was left alone. Under such circumstances, a cruel man took Rabia away and enslaved her.

Later on, for a small amount of money he sold her off. The person who bought her, gave her laborious tasks to do. One day, tired with the toils, Rabia fell down as she was going somewhere. One of her hands got hurt. In this condition Rabia bowed, prayed and for the first time addressed

God, "O, God, I was helpless and unprotected as it is. Now even my hand is broken. But I will accept your WILL. ...."

She then heard the divine voice, "Rabia, do not be downcast. You will attain that eminence and honour, that the rulers of your country will envy." This voice induced new life in her veins, she reached her master's house and engaged herself in serving him. During the day, she would fast and during the night, she would pray.

One night her master woke up from sleep. He saw to his surprise that a light was shining somewhere. Following this glow, he reached that corner where Rabia was praying. Radiance was spread around her. He even heard her voice. Rabia was speaking to God, "Had it been within my power, I would have spent all my time in praying to you. But you have made me someone else's servant. Therefore I get late to be in your service and prayer". Her employer was disturbed to hear this. He felt that he should have been serving that godly pious woman, whereas he was being attended by her. In the morning he gave her freedom from his service. So Rabia started coming out of the cell that she had thus made for herself in her employer's house. She would come out of that little room, sing His glory and be absorbed in divine instruction. Once Rabia set out to Mecca for Haj. On the way in her communication with God, she said, "God almighty, I am made of dust and the Kaba is made of stones. But I want to be in your presence, addressing you....".

She got the reply, "Rabia, let the custom of the world be as it is. Kohetoor was not able to stand my Radiance. He split into pieces. How will you be able to bear it?"

Rabia then said, "I do not need the abode but I need the dweller Himself. I desire the view of divine glory more than the glory of Kaba...".

That was the moment when the spiritual light illumined every fibre of Rabia.

Rabia-Leela

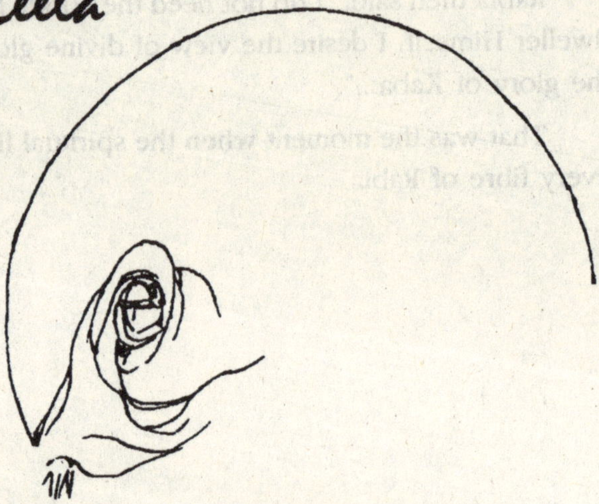

ONE EVENING, AS DARKNESS DESCENDED over dusk and as the fading light of the setting sun still lingered on, Rabia came out of her hut. She started searching for something in the dust.

The people around saw her groping in the ground and asked, "What is lost? Rabia, what are you looking for?"

She answered "I have lost my needle." They asked, "Where did you drop it?"

Rabia replied, "It fell somewhere inside the room...."

People laughed and said, "Rabia, are you out of your mind? Go inside and search. How can you find it out here?"

Rabia remarked, "I have always seen that people lose their God within themselves but are forever searching for Him outside themselves. So I can find my needle out here."

Just as sometimes Jesus had told his disciples, "You are the salt of this earth." Exactly in the same light, Osho refers to Rabia with an overwhelming heart —

"Rabia, you are the salt of all women that have existed and will ever exist on this earth."

Junaid

IN A CERTAIN VILLAGE, THERE lived a poor and honest man, who was always contemplating going to Mecca for Haj. He grew older and older till old age itself set in his very veins. As he could not find a friend to accompany him, he set out by himself for Haj, after collecting a meagre amount of money.

The journey was long and rigorous. He had no physical strength to go; but due to his keen devotion he somehow covered a part of the distance. On the way he met a sufi *dervesh*. Panting for breath, he asked the *dervesh*, "Miyan *dervesh*, how far is Mecca from here? How much further?"

This *dervesh* was Junaid, the saint of saints. He noticed that this good old man might die on the way only. So he told him, "Look, I shall tell you a secret. You stop here and go round me seven times and your Haj will be accomplished. Then, return to your village."

The old man heaved a sigh of relief. He went around Junaid seven times and was about to leave for his village when an idea struck him and he asked —

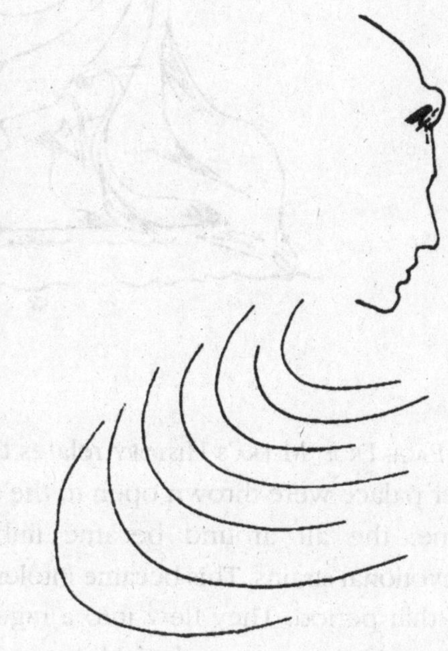

"Dervesh Miyan, if I have a longing to go for Haj once again and I do not meet you on the way, then what shall I do?"

Junaid said to him, "In that case, just go round yourself seven times. Your Haj will be solemnised."

Meera

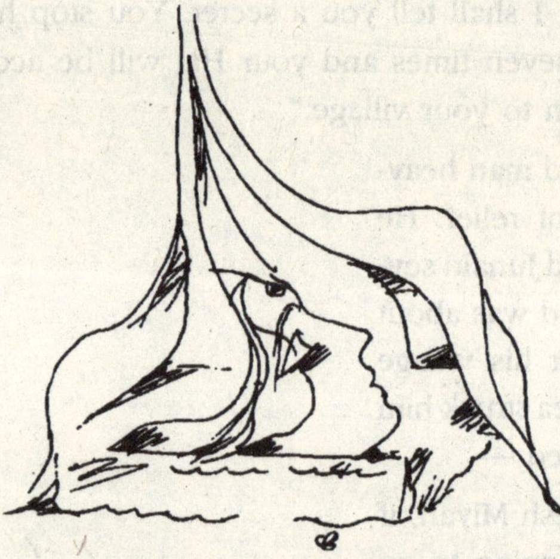

A Page From Meera's History relates this — When the gates of her palace were thrown open to the saints and hermits of that time, the air around became imbued with humans and devotional strains. This became intolerable for the conservatives of that period. They flew into a rage, as their eyes could not perceive the pure soul of Meera.

A conspiracy was hatched; that too in the name of God. A young Brahman lad was tempted and instigated to go to Meera. With blasphemy blatant on his lips, he uttered that he was commanded by God to enjoy Meera's bed for one night.

Meera simply listened to him and agreed. She asked him

to come in the evening. The young Brahman went home and got a silk attire ready. He decked himself up, wore scent and perfume and arrived at Meera's door in the evening.

The *durban* ushered him in, where Meera was engrossed in prayers and devotional songs with the saints and hermits. This youth noticed that in the middle, amongst the group of

Sadhus, a decorated bed was laid. His legs started trembling.

Meera saw this and said, "Come, the bed is ready..." The young man was dumbfounded. It was with difficulty that he stammered, "But in front of everyone....?"

Meera said, "Yes, God is everywhere and He sees everything. So from His saints I have nothing to hide. They too are manifestations of God himself."

The young man then fell at Meera's feet. He begged forgiveness which she alone could grant him. ... she alone, who was like a ray of God. ... .

Farid

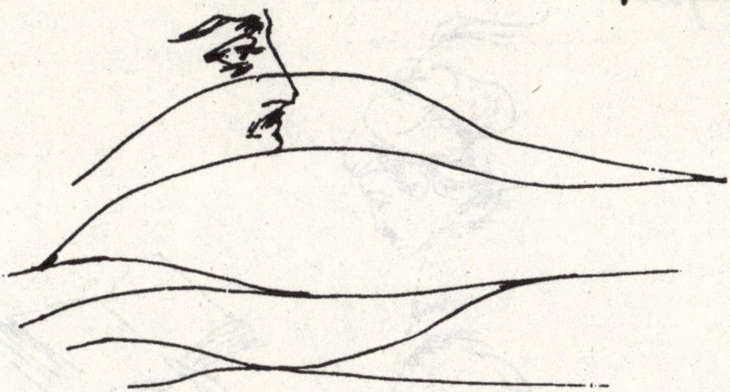

FARID WAS A SUFI *DERVESH*. The connoisseurs who heard his spiritual poetry became enthralled with it. The king who ruled then, was also desirous of his favourable glance. They say that the king once received a precious gift — golden scissors with diamonds studded on them. The king presented them to this peer, the holy man.

Farid held the scissors in his hand. Then returning them to the king he remarked, "If you have to make a presentation, O king! give me a needle, not scissors."

As the king was upset, Farid said, "The function of scissors is to cut; to turn into tatters an untorn cloth. But the object of a needle is to join rags. My purpose, O King! is similar to that of the needle and not of the scissors."

Sajda

THERE WAS A VERY LEARNED scholar of Arabic and Persian in Prince Muazzam's court in Delhi. He was Nandlal Goya. Once, the emperor Aurangzeb, the father of Prince Muazzam, desired that a particular stanza from the Qur'an be explained to him in full details. All the learned men of the court failed and the king was not convinced. Muazzam then said, "I know a scholar who can fathom the depth of the meanings." When Nandlal Goya came and explained to the satisfaction of the Emperor, the latter was elated. After Goya left, the king was highly perturbed that a Hindu scholar could reach the meanings that the Muslim learned men could not comprehend.

So he commanded that Nandlal Goya should be converted to Islam. Prince Muazzam regretted to have brought his friend to the royal court and realized that he had made a big mistake. Nandlal Goya said, "Where there is such an issue of being Hindu or Muslim, I cannot stay there any more."

Prince Muazzam knew his father well and also knew what would happen if his orders were not complied with. He arranged to secretly send Nandlal Goya far away so that he could not be heard of any more.

As he walked through a lonely path, Nandlal Goya cast away the question of a Hindu or a Muslim from his very being and looked up towards the sky. He laughed and gave his own identity—

"I have risen like a wave out of the full surging ocean, in order to salute and pay homage to MY OCEAN."

Rohion Wali

KHWAJA GHULAM FARID BELONGED To the Farruki family. His grandfather had come from Arabia and settled in Sindh, where he also held high posts and positions. But when the time came, he wore a *faqir*'s garb and adopted mendicant's life.

Maqdoom Muhammad Zikaria, who belonged to Sohravardi Sufi school of thinking, left Sindh and came to settle down in Muttan, where there were many Sufi *derveshes*. Even today the tomb of Maqdoom Noor Muhammad, who was from this very school of thinking, stands in *tehsil* Lodhran of Multan. The Emperor, Shah Jehan was also one of his devotees.

Khwaja Khuda Baksh was from this same family. Khwaja Farid was his son. Those with an insight recognized that the boy was chosen by God. When, after his father and his elder brother, he took the seat as Khwaja, he was wont to spend his whole night in meditation and praying.

Sufi *derveshes* generally choose the path of jungles or mountains but none knows the secret of how Ghulam Farid developed a passion for barren desolate lands. So much so that he spent eighteen years of his life in desolate wilderness where except for sand dunes there was no habitation.

In Chulstan, there is a place called Toba Bharavan where Khwaja Sahib pitched a tent and lived. There, a pretty lass would come grazing her sheep. Khwaja would come out of the tent to catch a glimpse of her. The name of that belle of those barren lands was Hoat.

They say that once some lambs climbed the scorching sand dune. Hoat got up and ran after them to bring them down. The afternoon was blazing hot. When Khwaja Sahib saw this from a distance he imagined Hoat's feet burning and ran behind her. He reached the sand dune and pulling off the chadar from his own shoulders, he provided shade over the head of Hoat Bibi...

It is believed that the seventh ray of the sun has an affinity with spiritual passion. It seems that at that moment the seventh ray of the sun manifested itself on that sand-dune.

Hoat Bibi's gaze was fixed on the radiant face of Khwaja Sahib.

When this news reached the group of shepherds, they rushed there with axes and choppers. But the ardent love of Rohion Wali remained everlasting. The shepherds performed the *nikah* of that belle of the barren lands with Khwaja Sahib.

The Woman of the Well

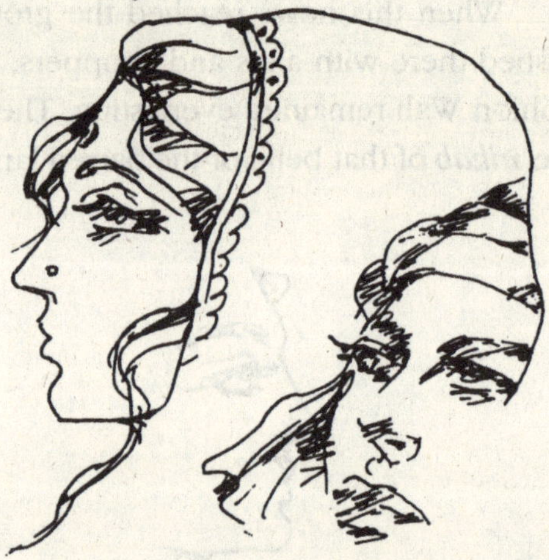

THERE USED TO BE A Faqir Sai in a village called Jagdeo in Punjab. People used to pray for their wishes and blessings to the tree under which he sat. There was a beautiful young girl in that village. When Faqir Sai saw her, he felt that he had experienced the view of God Himself. That pretty one, too, unmindful of rain or sun brought sweets hidden by her veil and presented to Faqir Sai as her offering.

This offering conveyed her loving devotion. At this, the villagers expressed blazing anger because the *Faqir* was a Muslim and the girl was a Hindu belonging to an affluent family. Hence Faqir Sai had to leave the village.

They say that there were three approaches to the village. In summer not a drop of water was available for travellers to drink. Faqir Sai wandered away to unknown distant paths. That beautiful girl got wells dug on all three roads and she herself started offering drinking water to passers-by.

As the season of youth declined, Faqir Sai once passed that way. The woman serving water to drink recognized him and offered him a bowl-full. When Faqir Sai, too, recalled that ethereal face, the pangs of separation of the life-time, trembled on his quivering lips. A smile lit her face when she told him, "It was my longing to see you which inspired me to recognize the thirst of the way-side-travellers. Even as they quench their thirst with cool water, I feel a contentment within me as though I have really seen you."

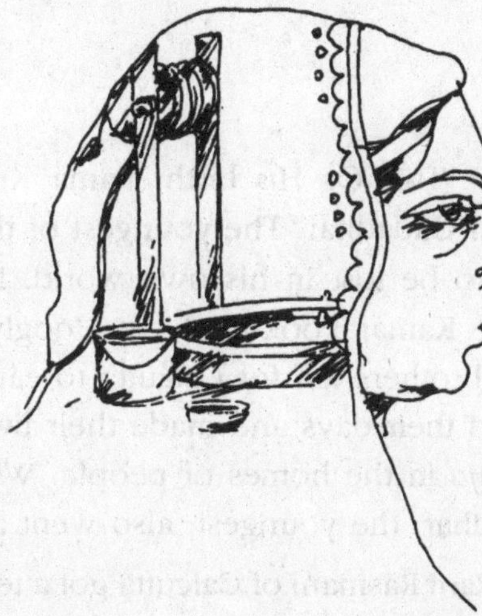

Nobody knows her name even now. She was called *Kuen Wali* then and even today when they mention her they remember her as *Kuen Wali*, the Woman of the Well.

Rama Krishna

At The Time Of His birth, Rama Krishna Param Hans was named Gadadhar. The youngest of three brothers, Gadadhar used to be lost in his own world. He was born in a small village Kamar Pookur of the Hoogly district in Bengal. His elder brothers left for Calcutta to earn their livelihood. They passed their days and made their living by performing *Thakurpuja* in the homes of people. When he grew up a little, Gadadhar, the youngest, also went and joined his brothers.

Rani Rasmani of Calcutta got a temple of Mehamaya built in the garden of her house on the bank of Ganga. She appointed Gadadhar's elder brother as the priest. Later on

Gadadhar became the priest.

By now, Gadadhar came to be known as Rama Krishna. His spontaneous devotion for Devi which was his inclination by birth opened the portals of his mind. Through them he entered the light of spiritualism. All rituals and religious practices were left behind. All by himself, wandering amongst the energy-fragment, Ram Krishna became a fragment of energy himself.

His brothers got him married to a pretty six-year-old girl, Sharda, in order to bind him to the worldly life. Many a time he seated Sharda in the place of Devi and started worshipping her...

Often, while he offered her the puja-flowers, he would strew them on his own head. When the inner fragrance merged with the fragrance of these flowers, he was steeped in the divine light as he sang and danced in raptures. He eagerly longed to see his Devi Ma in a living form. So he would call out and cry at times. This eagerness became more and more expressive and often he was heard to be in conversation with Devi. Every morning he used to pluck flowers for *Puja* from the garden below. A time came when he could no longer bring himself to break the flowers which were happily swinging in the branches. The complaint was made as expected, that Rama Krishna did not offer flowers to Devi any more and so the Puja remained incomplete. Rama Krishna then laughed and said, "I do offer flowers to Devi. I worship her with flowers. Then all the flowers that bloom in this garden, I offer to her, her alone, in prayer."

Ma Sharda

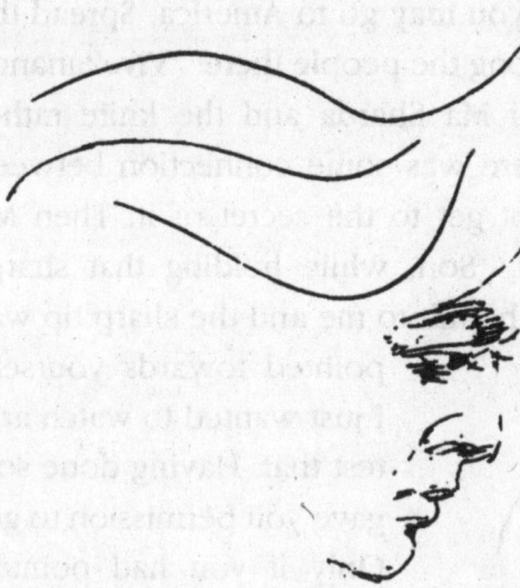

PARAM HANS RAMA KRISHNA HAD that inner experience which is bestowed on one after many a century. But he was not endowed with the talent of speech. Vivekananda possessed the knowledge of *Shastras* as well as the gift of speech. Rama Krishna passed energy to Vivekananda and gave him the profound glimpse of experience. He prepared him to carry the message of spirituality to the distant parts of the world through his voice.

When Vivekananda was ready to leave for America, he went to seek permission from his Guru-mother Sharda. At the time Ma Sharda was in the kitchen. She said, "Son, there is a knife on that high shelf in front. Just pass it to me." Vivekananda took that knife down and gave it to Ma Sharda. Ma, then said, "Yes, son, you may go to America. Spread the message of your Guru among the people there." Vivekananda viewed the permission of Ma Sharda and the knife rather curiously. He felt that there was some connection between the two. But he could not get to the secret of it. Then Ma Sharda laughed and said, "Son, while holding that sharp-edged knife, you offered the hilt to me and the sharp tip was pointed towards yourself. I just wanted to watch and test that. Having done so I gave you permission to go. Only if you had pointed the handle to me and the sharp edge towards yourself, would I have permitted you. The question is of PEOPLE and not of ME. You will be able to present them simple experience and you yourself will protect them from all kinds of doubts and the piercing blades of arguments. So I have said, "Son, you go!"

The Destined Meeting

SHAH LATIF HAD A PRE-DESTINED meeting with Sayyada Bibi, one which threw open for him the way – that of mendicants – of poetry as well as the call of God.

The piece of land which is called Sindh, at one time, used to be the abode of Sufi mendicants. The grandfather of Shah Abdul Latif too came from Hirat and settled in Sindh.

Shah Abdul Latif, owing to whose writings of the Sufi poetry in Sindhi is famous today, was born in 1689 in the house of Shah Habib, who was wont to lead a mendicant's life. He was taught Arabic and Persian and became a scholar in his mother tongue, Sindhi. He lived in a village named

Kotri.

Here, in Kotri, there was a wealthy Moghul, Mirza Moghul Beg. His daughter fell ill, so he sent for Sayyad Dervesh Shah Habib, to give spiritual treatment. It so chanced that Shah Habib was rather unwell and therefore he sent his young son Shah Latif to offer prayers. When he saw Sayyada Bibi, he was enthralled by her bewitching beauty. Since he had come to cure her, he took control of himself. Holding a finger of Sayyada, he read the prayers.

Mirza Moghul Beg was standing beside him, and all this was disagreeable to him. At the time he kept quiet but later he swore enmity with the Sayyads. The Sayyads were driven to such a state that in utter helplessness they were compelled to leave Kotri; and outside the town they raised walls in an open space and started living there. Shah Latif, immersed in the spirit of renunciation, would go and sit in desolate ruins or mounds of sand and would get engrossed in the servitude of God. Once it happened that oblivious of the sand-storm, he got buried under a dune. However the corner of his shawl was sticking out. A shepherd noticed it and pulled Shah Latif out of the sand. Every course for him was obstructed by silence. Hence Shah Latif mingled with a group of *yogis* and left on a long journey. He went to the temple of Kali. He also met great enlightened faqirs and derveshes. He visited Bambhor and penned down the love legend of *Sassi.* Then he went to the temple of Hingla Devi, where people bathe the idol of Parvati with milk. He saw the cave of Lahut where milk trickles from stones resembling cow's udders. This place is known as *Gokul* in this area. All these particles of cosmic energy were transforming into Shah Latif's poetic diction.

On the other side, nature took a fateful turn. There was a dacoity in Mirza Moghul Beg's house. Wealth was robbed but his haughtiness still remained. When Mirza chased the dacoits, the Sayyads wanted to help but the conceited Mirza refused the offer. He himself and all the people with whom he was following the robbers were killed in the jungles. In the house of the Moghuls there was raised a hue and cry to be saved and protected.

They considered that the enmity they had nurtured with the Sayyads had become a curse from God. So to the house of Sayyads, now they sent a proposal of marriage of Sayyada Bibi to Shah Latif... and this destined meeting became a destined union...

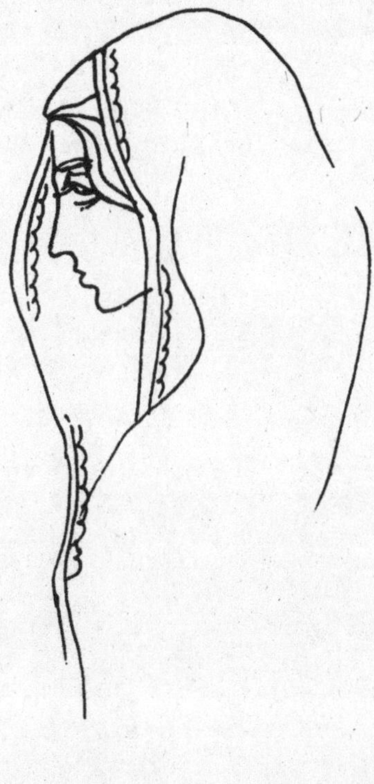

Shah Latif was a *Karmyogi dervesh*. His disciples would offer countless gifts. But Shah Latif and Sayyada Begum would distribute all that wealth among the needy. The expenses of their own living were managed with the land they owned. Sayyada Begum was a daughter of a Moghul family and was brought up amidst much affluence. But after being united to Shah Latif, she herself adopted the life of a *dervesh*.

Ranka - Banka

THERE IS AN ANCIENT STORY of Maharashtra. A lovable soul in the shape of Ranka was born in Pandarpur. Only simplicity of life was acceptable to Ranka even in his childhood. So much so that poverty at home drove him to the roads of the jungle everyday to collect drywood. This was his only job. He brought dry wood from the forest and sold it in the market. This job was his only means of earning his daily bread. When he grew up to be a young man, Banka, a pretty girl became his wife. Now both of them would go to the woods together, happily singing away. They would rustle along, the breeze blowing in the trees of the jungle, pick wood, tie it, place it on their heads and return to the village.

Once, they were coming back as usual when Ranka, who was walking much ahead spied a bag full of gold coins. He put down the bundle from his head quickly. He then dug a hole in the ground, placed the bag inside and covered it up with earth.

Hardly had he got up and lifted the bundle on to his head when Banka reached. She asked him, "What is it? What are you doing Ranka?"

Ranka fell silent. He wasn't wont to speak anything but truth. Hence he had to tell her, "There was a bag of gold coins. I was hiding it in the ground, so that your mind does not get swayed."

Banka is said to have laughed a full hearty laugh. Ranka wondered, "Why this laughter, Banka?"

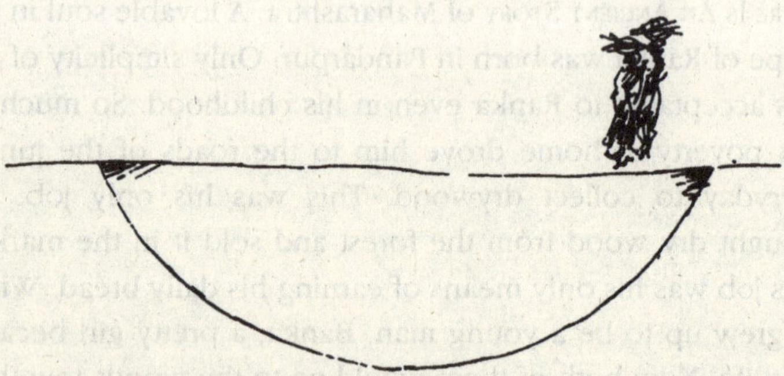

She just replied, "I am laughing to see that under the dust you have hidden merely dust."

Ranka had always felt a spirit of detachment and renunciation. But in renunciation, a door still 'remains', and in detachment there remains a realization of attachment. Whereas, Banka had stepped beyond renunciation and detachment. For her, gold or dust had the same significance. The reddish glow of the setting sun lit up her forehead. Under that glow, Ranka could not restrain himself. He embraced Banka with such loving reverence as though his own being was bowing in absolute salutation to her.

Uttara-Shankar

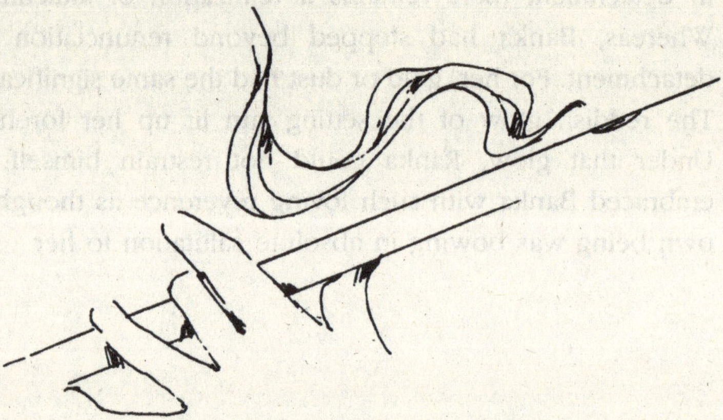

A Story About Uttara And Shankar is told in the hilly regions of Punjab. Uttara was said to be so beautiful that when anyone saw her, one imagined that somebody from this earth had artfully deceived and lured her from the city of gods....

When she grew up to be a young girl, she took the goats to graze on the hills. While passing through the neighbouring village, she happened to fall in love with a young shepherd from there. His name was Shankar.

For quite sometime, there had been some friction between the two tribes of Uttara and Shankar. So it posed a problem for both of them. At nightfall, she would hear the sound of Shankar's flute, floating over the mountains. Much as people at home checked and stopped her, Uttara would run as if it were winged feet.

Both the tribes, they say, were so enraged that one day Shankar renounced everything and just went away with the *yogis*. *Yogis* have neither fixed places nor destinations. Uttara sent messages to him many times through passers-by. Yet there was no news of him.

Only once, a traveller brought back a reply. "Uttara, my heart has now become a straw in the storm. At present these cruel winds are blowing, carrying the straw along with them."

Uttara is said to have given the bangles from her wrist to this traveller and requested him to give this message to Shankar —

"O, Straw, my Sai,

Whisper into the ears of the storms,

Blow hither,

Blow towards Uttara."

And the story goes that when it snowed on the hillside, Uttara stood on a hillock waiting for Shankar. He did come. The whole village heard the sound of his flute. After this no one in the village ever saw them return. Many years have passed since, no one knows how many! Even now, some can hear the sound of a flute floating from across the mountains.

The Hafiza

In The Kashmiri Language, A prostitute is called *hafiza*. Once a beautiful *hafiza* was going through hard times. She was all alone and was left helplessly lonely. So from the region of Tashwan, crossing the river Vitsala she went to a renowned *acharya* of his times, Shri Ram. She went to him to ask for a wish and be blessed. Shri Ram was a scholar of Agam Shastra and his legs lost the capacity to walk due to his sitting in meditation for many years. He would just sit on the *asan*, a small carpet in the *ashram* and would teach Agam Shastra to the seekers.

"Come, daughter," uttering this when he consoled the *hafiza*, it is said that all of a sudden her luck changed. A certain wealthy man of Gilgit came, who heard her sing a sufi song, saw her dance and he gifted his entire treasury to her. hafiza Full of gratitude, the *hafiza* went to the Ashram of Shri Ram with offerings of dry fruits and touched his feet.

Shri Ram picked up one almond and kept it on his *asan*. Giving her a few gold coins he told her, "I cannot accept anything from a daughter's house. The daughter has come all the way, therefore, I must give you a token present." The *hafiza* tearfully said, "Just grant me my desire. Please hear me sing a sufi song. My soul is in it."

Shri Ram fixed up the next day for this. He called all his disciples and hermits and said, "Tomorrow in the evening Sham Sundari Sharika is coming here. If you look at her with purity in your mind and intention, you shall be blessed with whatever you desire." The *Para-Shakti* of Shri Chakra is called Sharika Sham Sundari. So the disciples were quite surprised. The next day when the *hafiza* sang the sufi song which penetrated the soul of the listeners, the hermits actually felt that in the form of the *hafiza*, they indeed had the revered glimpse of Sharika Sham Sundari.

All the dry fruits were distributed among the disciples and they felt that they were all graced with beneficence.

In the memory of this episode, Shri Ram Trik ashram exists in Fatehakdal even to this day, though all this happened one hundred and fifty years ago. It is also believed that one day Sharika Sham Sundari actually appeared there in person.

Sai Bulleshah

ONCE A SUFI DERVESH, SAI Bulleshah was sitting in his secluded cell and was praying. His disciples were squatting outside, eating carrots. Some Muslims who were observing religious fast happened to walk past them. When they saw his followers eating carrots, they stopped and asked in enraged tones, "Eh! Don't you know that this is the month of Ramzan?"

The disciples just nodded in reply meaning, "Well! So what?"

The fasting men thought that these might not be Muslims. So, for their own satisfaction they asked, "Which community do you belong to?"

Those people casually said, "Mussalmans."

At this, the fasting men became infuriated. There and then, they started hitting and beating them. It struck them that they ought to see in what state the saint of these disciples was. So they entered the cell and asked Bulleshah, who was sitting in prayer, "What are you?". Bulleshah raised his arms and gesticulated to convey that he didn't know.

They again roared and questioned him, "Why don't you speak? What community do you belong to?"

Bulleshah again put up his arms and waved his hands. Those people took him to be a madman, left him alone and went their own way.

After they were gone, the disciples raved and ranted and came to Bulleshah. They showed him the blue marks on their legs and arms. Bulleshah asked them, "What did you tell them?" They replied, "Nothing! We only said that were Muslims......"

Bulleshah smiled and said, "See! you claimed to be something. As a result you were beaten up, I denied being anything so I escaped the beating." And Bulleshah, in rapturous ecstasy, burst into singing :

"Realize do I ....

The beginning and the end am I,

There is none else than I,

Bulleshah, say, who **is** *WHO?*

How can I, Bullia know.......

I am WHO?"

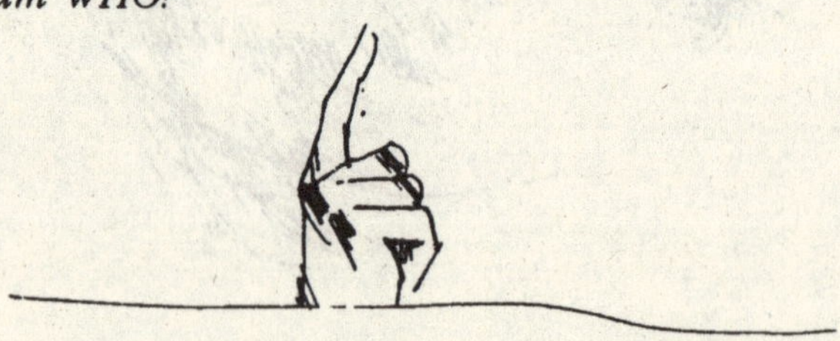

Kingship

Sai Bulleshah Happened To Pass through some place in a carefree, unconcerned mood, oblivious of everything.

Some people surrounded and questioned him, "Well, who are you?"

Bulleshah said, "I am a King."

These very words were quoted to the king who ruled at that time.

"A beggar calls himself a king. He disregards you."

Bulleshah was summoned to the king's court and interrogated, "Sir, beggar, you call yourself a king!"

Bullesah replied, "I do not call myself a king. I am a King."

They ridiculed him and asked, "Kings have armies,.ready at all time. Where is your army?"

Bulleshah laughed, "Those kings who are enemies of certain people and who themselves have many enemies, keep an army. But I am nobody's foe nor do I have any. Then why should I possess an army? Whatever for?"

Bulleshah glanced up at the sky and said, "The monarchs of this world need to have subjects. But the *derveshes* of God are monarchs themselves and they themselves are the subjects."

Pooran Sanyasi

Pooran Singh Has Been Characteristically a *dervesh* poet of Punjabi. Noticing his intellectual capabilities, his family had sent him to Japan for higher studies. When he returned from Japan, Pooran happened to meet Swami Ram Teerth.

He became immersed in the colour of *derveshi* and Pooran Singh clad himself in saffron robes. Much before leaving for Japan, at an early age, his betrothal to Maya had taken place. From her writings, we gather that when she was ten years old, she used to pray to Gauri. Sometime during these prayers, within herself, she accepted Shiva as her Lord So when she was engaged to Pooran, he appeared to her entirely as Lord Shiva himself.

When he was returning from Japan, preparations had already begun at home, for the wedding. At that time nature took a strange turn. Pooran had met Swami Ram Teerthjee. Quite unexpectedly, Maya's brother received a letter from him that he had become a *sanyasi.* Pooran bade him to marry his sister off to someone else. Those days, girls never argued with their fathers or elder brothers but even at that time Maya said, "My marriage with Pooran has already been solemnized. If you compel me, I shall end my life......."

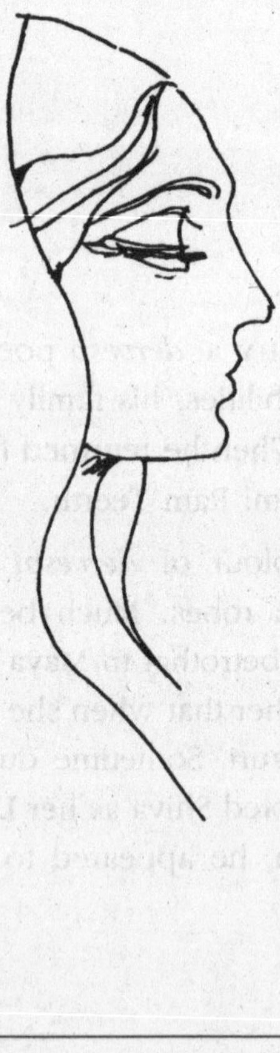

Pooran's parents went to Calcutta. They located and brought him back. Somehow or the other, they were able to take him to Mayadevi's house in Peshawar. Pooran met Maya and told her, "I have become a *Faqir.* If you too want to become a *Faqir,* then do as you wish." That time Maya readily agreed to be a *Faqir.*

Pooran said, "You will have to beg for alms." Maya said, "Yes, I will."

It is then that Pooran said to her, "If it be so, do get up and come with me."

Hazrat Inayat Khan

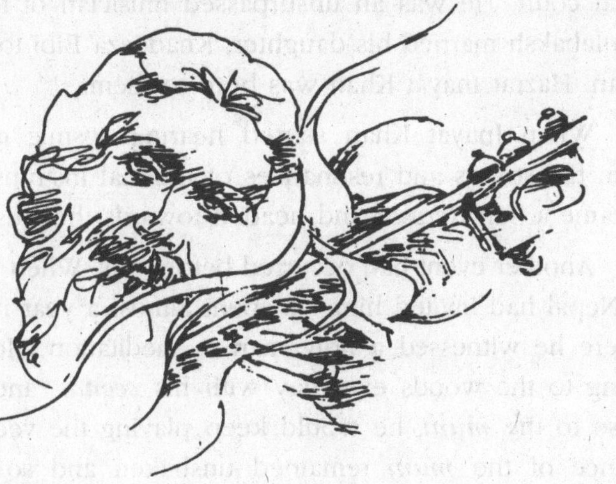

In Delhi, At A Distance of a few furlongs from the *dargah* of Hazrat Nizamuddin Aulia, is the *dargah* of the musician, Hazrat Inayat Khan. This is written on his tomb—

Hazrat Peer-o-Murshid Inayat Khan

The Founder of Sufi wave in the west

5th July 1882— 9th February 1927.

Rahmat Khan was from Sialkot. He received his training in music from Peer Iliyas, who was *dervesh* as well as an expert in Dhrupad. When Rahmat Khan came of age, he renounced his home and set out. A certain devoted godman in Ajmer indicated to him that he should go to Baroda.

When he went to Baroda, he met Maulabaksh of the royal court. He was an unsurpassed musician of the time. Maulabaksh married his daughter, Khadeeza Bibi to Rahmat Khan. Hazrat Inayat Khan was born to them.

When Inayat Khan started hearing cosmic mysteries from the strings and resonances of musical instruments, he became a Sufi *dervesh* and headed towards the west.

Another event had occurred before this. When the King of Nepal had invited him, he spent almost a year in Nepal, where he witnessed a holy man in meditation. He started going to the woods everyday with his *veena;* and, sitting close to the *muni*, he would keep playing the veena. The silence of the *muni* remained unshaken and so did his meditation. This was a divine experience. Inayat Khan writes, "It felt as though a curtain lifted off from the riddles of the musical notes."

During his adolescence, something else had happened. In his dream, he would see some angelic face which he never got to see in real life. Once he chanced to go to Hyderabad, where he got an audience with Sayyad Mohammad Abu Hashim Madni. He recognized the ethereal face that he used to see in his dreams. It was this meeting that steeped Hazrat Inayat Khan in the Sufi hue. He received the same message from his master.

"Take the Sufi spirit to the west." He went to the west

and started a journal called 'Sufi'. He continued presenting a Sufi point of view in the musical concerts as well.

In 1923, he went to America via London and France. When he was questioned by the immigration authorities, his replies were —

"Place of birth?"

"This world."

"Religion?"

"All religions."

"Profession?"

"Quest for Truth. Service of the Lord and humanity."

Mikhail Naimy

'THE BOOK OF MIR DAD' is one of those books in the world which are very rarely revealed to the chosen few.

Mikhail Naimy was born in 1889 in Lebanon, in a village surrounded by mountains on three sides. Leading the life of a *dervesh*, as a youth, Naimy wrote many books full of sensitive inner experiences in his own language, Arabic. But when he was endowed with the revelation of this one, he wrote it in English, 'The Book of Mir Dad' and translated it later in his own tongue, Arabic. None of the mysteries of this book can be grasped. One can merely say that each and every line of it appears to be drawing towards the lofty peaks of consciousness.

It is a matter of myth; the myth that is dormant in the inner consciousness of every human being. Among the milky white mountains, there is a high peak which is known as Puja Choti, the peak of worship. There is a sad and vast ruin of a monastery which is known as Noah's Ark.

A legend goes among the dwellers of this hill that after the doom of the great flood, Hazrat Noah and his family had come there. During that time, the land here was fertile and the lakes and rivers were full and flowing. When the last days of Noah drew near, he told his son to make a prayer-room so that with the passage of time people did not forget the story of the great flood. He said, "The prayer-room should be in the shape of an ark and the fire lit there should burn forever." He also added, "My son, here you must make a hermitage for nine people. This number should never exceed nor become less......"

When Hazrat Noah breathed his last, his son obeyed all his commands. He buried Hazrat Noah under the prayer room and lighted an eternal flame too. People from the valley's would come, see the prayer-room, make offerings of sesame and flowers and would be blessed with spiritual indications.

Centuries took a turn and the nine priests began taking land, gold and silver from the people. The prayer-hall got richer and people became poorer.

Of those nine leaders, one died. Then as per instructions, they started waiting for some one to come and substitute that position. By chance a stranger with radiance in his eyes came to take that place. But the chief straightaway rejected when he saw him and declared that he would not be accepted. However, the others melted with compassion and the stranger was made to stay on as an attendant.

Gradually as some years passed, the chief came to know that the settlements sprawling for miles, that were owned by him, were getting disorderly and scattered. The companions of the chief getting tired of the rules and regulations, started taking guidance from that stranger. They made the farmer-workers the owners of their land. A curse fell on the chief. He lost his speech and they say that solitary like a spectre, he got stuck to the hilly tracks.

This folk-legend becomes even more significant. When a genuine seeker went to that hill of hard and difficult roads, the chief haunting the hill-side confessed his sins to him. He informed him that the legend that went round the villages of that hill was true. He admitted that when the stranger had come, he himself was the captain of Noah's ark. He had possessed countless riches, but when he saw the radiance of that stranger, daggers of jealousy had pierced his heart, He had wished to kill him and finish him. He had felt that this was some godly soul which would uncover the veil hiding his own sins. His arrogance had made him blind. He said, "I did not want to be humiliated in the presence of this stranger, so

I started humiliating him."

"His name was Mir Dad. He was appointed as an attendant but by and by, he became the master of the people. I resorted to treacheries beyond limits but he had made his place in the hearts of the people. Besides, he distributed the entire wealth of the monastery among the people. This tied my tongue. I became almost an apparition."

There in the cave lay the book, which was written about Mir Dad by a friend of his. Giving the information of this book to this seeker, the chief left his haunted body forever!

Mir Dad

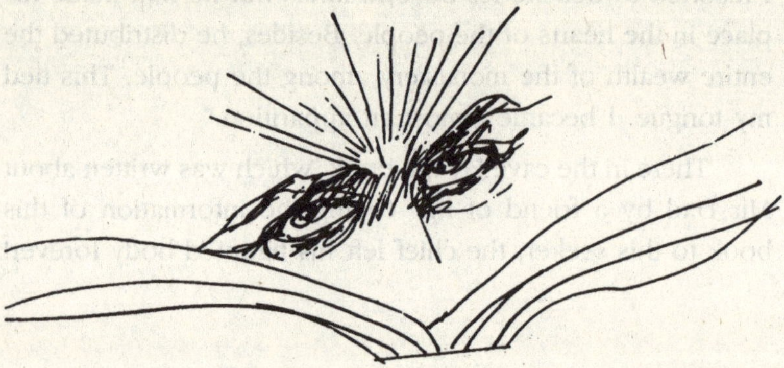

When Cosmic Consciousness Made Mikhail Naimy the medium of its voice, Mir Dad became the symbol of his writings, the character of Mikhail Naimy's tale, 'The Book of Mir Dad.'

The companions of Mir Dad considered him their master; and these seekers were thirsting for answers. As though they were the symbols of quest, they posed certain questions.

The answers of those questions by Mir Dad are replete with the same spiritual consciousness that was bestowed upon the author, Mikhail Naimy, as a revelation.

Mir Dad tells his friends, "Whenever your lips pronounce

'I', that very moment say in your heart, "Oh! God, protect me from the distresses of 'I' and show me the path, so that enjoy the bliss of 'I'".

"Silent and devoid of body, 'I' is the consciousness of your being. That has been embodied by giving it a voice. Whatever is within you that is inaudible, may be heard; and that is invisible, may be seen.

"'I' is a magic wand. But even a magical wand cannot give birth to something which the magician does not possess. As the magician is, similar kind of objects can the wand produce. Hence, as your consciousness is, likewise is you 'I'. As your 'I' is, likewise is your world.

"A human being is a wandering cloud with God embedded within him. Till such time that he empties himself, he cannot find himself."

By such discourse Mir Dad tells us that he imparted

similar learning to Noah and that is what he is teaching us too.

These words make Mir Dad infinite and limitless, and become the 'manifestation' of Timeless Consciousness.

Once, one of his companions, soaked in astonishment asked him, "Mir Dad, who are you?"

His reply was, "When I am among the human beings, I am God and when I am with God, I am a human being."

A Sadhu

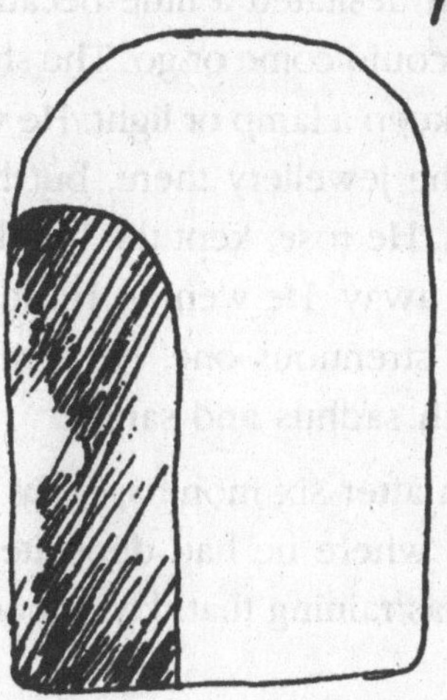

THERE WERE A NUMBER OF camps of *sadhus* across the railway line in the city of Gujranwala. On this side of the railway line, lived the people with families and households. Many of them used to visit the camps of sadhus in the morning, with flowers, *batashas*, flour and lentils.

One of these residents was a regular visitor to a particular tent. One day, he touched the Sadhu's feet and placed a small bundle containing jewellery and said, "Maharaj, I entrust this bundle in your charge. I have to go to Haridwar. It may be months before I return. I'll come back and take it from you."

The Sadhu said, "Keep it there in the alcove in that wall in front." That man hesitated a little because it was an open camp and anyone could come or go. The shelf was open. May be it was made to keep a lamp or light. He wondered whether he should leave the jewellery there, but had no courage to disobey the Sadhu. He rose, kept the bundle in that recess in the wall and went away. He went to Haridwar. In those days the journey was a strenuous one. He went to Rishikesh and kept company with sadhus and saints.

On his return after six months, early in the morning he went to the camp where he had deposited the bundle with the Sadhu. As it was raining that day, other devotees had not yet arrived.

He offered his namaskar to the Sadhu, sat near his feet and reminded him, "Maharaj, I had left a bundle with you. It contained jewellery. I have now come to take that back."

That Sadhu looked here and there with vacant eyes which had no trace of recollection of any such thing. He said, "I do not remember."

That man got really worried. He thought to himself, "I am done for! All that I have earned in my life time is lost." Then he helped the Sadhu to recall.. "You were sitting here, on this asan; it was wrapped in a red piece of cloth, tied with a black thread." The Sadhu merely said, "But when?"

This person's heart sank. He uttered in a broken voice, "About six months back."

As the sadhu looked at him with surprise, he added, "Maharaj, try and recall. You had asked me to keep the bundle in that recess in the wall, so I obeyed you and kept it in that alcove." The Sadhu laughed. "Was it a matter to remember! If you had kept the bundle in the alcove, go and ask the alcove. Why are you asking me?"

Scared and trembling, that person went to the wall and groped. There the bundle was, in a corner of the alcove.

This man was embarrassed and came to the Sadhu with folded hands. He appealed, "I was wrong, O holy one; suspicion crept into my mind. I do not know how to thank you."

The Sadhu laughed and said, "If you have done something wrong, ask the alcove to forgive you. It kept your deposit so very safely. And if you want to offer your thanks, then thank the alcove."

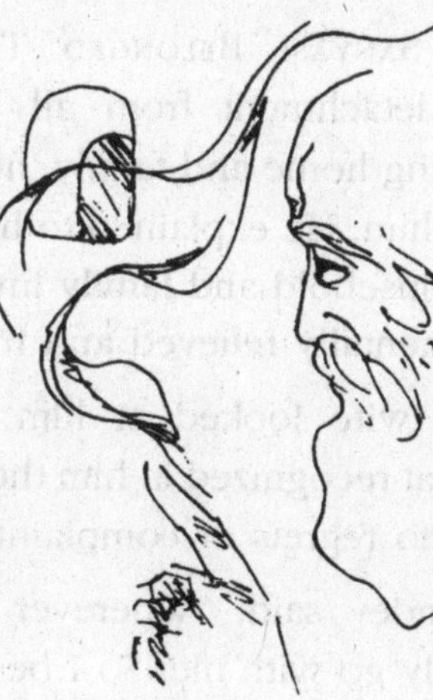

Ramdev Sanyasi

Ramdev Sanyasi Belonged To Gujranwala. He felt a certain detachment from all wordly desires. Just before renouncing home and family, he made his wife sit down and listen to him. He explained to her that his heart was no more in the household and family involvements. But he was keen to feel mentally relieved and free to leave home.

His wife looked at him with tearful eyes. She had somewhat recognized in him the spirit that he was steeped in. Hence, no regrets or complaints came to her lips.

Ramdev said, "Wherever I go, concern for you will constantly go with me. So I beseech you to help me. Please deliver me of this worry."

His wife was both surprised and grateful for his deep concern for her. She said, "Take me along with you. I shall also become a sanyasin." Ramdev said, "*Sanyas*, my dear, is a state of mind. It is not a compulsion of circumstances."

His wife could not grasp the depth of what he said. So he elaborated, "I have a close friend. If only you too like him, I wish to marry you off to him, myself." His wife got confused with the thoughts of sins and virtues.

So Ramdev said, "The man whom you married is no more here. I am not 'he'. Hence the thought of good or bad should not even enter your mind."

Next day, the people of the town were wonderstruck to see that Ramdev was present at the wedding ceremony and he himself gave away the bride in marriage. He left everything, house, money and jewellery to her.

Ramdev clad himself in saffron coloured robes and carried on.

A Faqir Sai

THERE USED TO BE A *Faqir* Sai, who had built a hut for himself outside the village. Passers by used to bow their heads to him. He was regarded as an elevated soul, doing noble work.

It so happened that in the village, an unmarried girl delivered a baby. Abuses were showered on her and out of fear, she gave the name of this *dervesh* as being responsible for the child.

Her parents and others were boiling with rage. Their curses and abuses were now directed to Sai's hut. The girl's father filled with anger, along with some other men came to *Faqir* Sai . Dropping the baby in his lap, he told him, "Hold it in your own hands. It is yours."

Sai saw the wailing child and muttered, "Oh? Is it mine?" The baby was crying bitterly for milk. But Sai had no means to buy milk. He clutched the baby to his heart and holding the *kaskaul* and the *kamandal*, he went around the village asking for milk.

People would close their doors on his face as soon as they saw him. Nobody wanted to see either his face or the child's.

There was this one house among others, where no sooner were the shrieks of this baby heard, than a young girl ran and sprung the door open. She fell at Sai's feet, "O, good man, I just took your name to conceal the real one. It was a lie, O, great noble soul, today every door in the village has

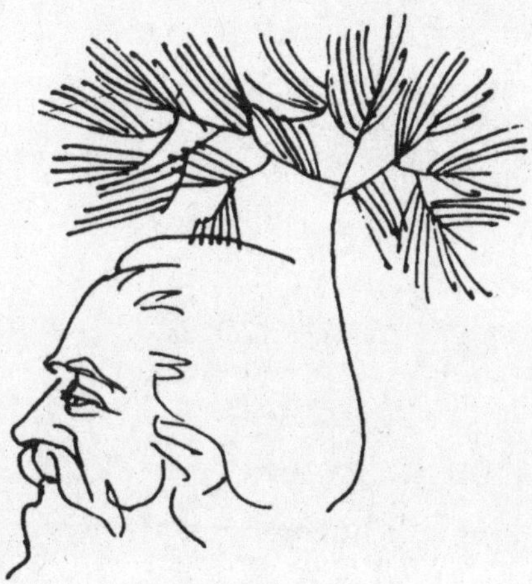

been closed on you. O, do forgive me." Then the girl took the child from Faqir Sai and clasping it to her bosom, she started feeding the baby.

The villagers again gathered. Her father was really ashamed and with a gaze full of remorse, he could only bow his head and look at Sai's feet. "We are sinners, Oh Sai, that we laid the blame on you. No! this baby is not yours."

It is said that *Faqir* Sai could utter no more than the words "O, is it not mine?" AND..... he simply went away.

A Dervesh

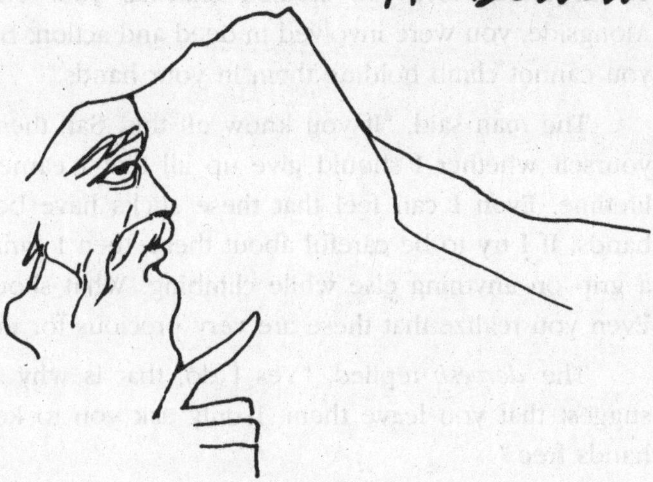

ONCE SOMEONE WAS TRYING To climb a steep hill carrying two big sticks with both his hands. He was finding it difficult — both feet slipping, hand unable to find a hold. He was clutching on to the sticks desperately and trying his very best. He was gasping for breath when a *dervesh* passed by. He said, "O, good man, both your hands are occupied. You cannot ascend like this."

That man looked up with tired eyes and told the *dervesh*, "Sai, do you mean that I should throw away these sticks? You do not know that I have spent my whole life acquiring these." The *dervesh* said, "I do know it. One of these sticks represents knowledge and the other philosophy. To acquire these, you studied Shastras your entire life. Alongside, you were involved in deed and action. But surely you cannot climb holding them in your hands."

The man said, "If you know all this, Sai, then tell me yourself whether I should give up all that I earned in my lifetime. Even I can feel that these sticks have bound my hands. If I try to be careful about them, then I cannot have a grip on anything else while climbing. What should I do? Even you realize that these are very precious for me."

The *dervesh* replied, "Yes I do, that is why I do not suggest that you leave them. I only ask you to keep your hands free."

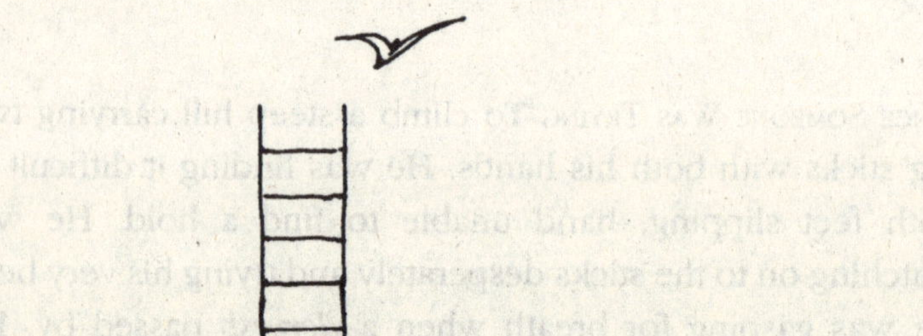

The man laughed and said, "These *derveshes* are mad people. On one hand, he asks me to free my hands. At the same time, he claims that he is not telling me to throw the sticks away."

It was the *dervesh* who laughed this time and remarked, "Good man, both the things I said are absolutely correct. Make the two sticks, the two sides of the steps. Between them, just fit in small twigs of your experiences at short distances. This will provide you splendid stairs. Thus you will climb the entire height of the slope very fast."

Blavatskaya

Osho Tells Us About Blavatskaya. She is the only woman on this earth who ever started a religion. She is the founder of 'Theosophy'. Her book 'Secret Doctrine' is a collection of cosmic secrets which she had compiled by journeying all over the world. She lived in Tibet for a considerably long time. However, she has also collected some unnecessary material from elsewhere. But in certain places in her writings, diamonds are strewn.

Her full name is Elena Petrovna Blavatskaya. She was born in Russia in 1831. Her mother Elena was a novelist and her father, a colonel. At the age of seventeen, she was married. Marriage, to her, was a binding restriction. Therefore she left for America, passing through Turkey, Greece and Canada. From there she came to India and proceeded to Tibet in 1857. Once she even visited Russia. In the course of her next journey, she went to New York and it was in 1875 that she founded the Theosophical Society. Her purpose was

to know the particles of spiritual energy which form the unit of this entire universe. She aimed to give an identity to that human point of view where there are no distinctions of race or religion. To know that law of nature which has blended and assimilated itself in the human being; which is inexplicable and invisible but which can only be lived. She came to India again and laid a permanent location for this line of thinking and its study, in Madras, in 1883. Later on, branches in Germany and London were also established.

Blavatskaya, who gave to the world the philosophy of seven races, was known for her profound sensitivity too. Due to this, wherever she went, she would fill a bag with various seeds of flowers suitable for that season and would sling it on her shoulder. Wherever she found good soil for the flowers, she would scatter and sprinkle the seeds. Often people would tell her, "Blavatskaya you have sown the flowers today. When they grow and bloom, you won't be there to see, as your feet are always on the move on new paths. Why do you take so much trouble?"

She would reply, "Friends, when the flowers blossom, I shall not be. But thousands of people will be here to look at the flowers."

Hazrat Baba Tajuddin Aulia

HAZRAT BABA TAJUDDIN AULIA WAS a *dervesh* from whom numerous people received spiritual grace as well as fulfilment of their worldly wishes.

In the event of the Congress session held in Nagpur in 1920, many leaders like Jawaharlal Nehru, Shaukat Ali, Maulana Abdul Kalam Azad, Sardar Vallabh Bhai Patel and Lokmanya Tilak went to Baba Tajuddin to take blessings for the freedom of the country.

On another occasion, Baba had told Gandhiji, "Sir, if only you had kept a basket and a broom on your head everything would have been set right." Taking this hint,

Gandhiji started the Harijan movement.

In Vardha, Shri Hanumanta Rao Naidu was a great follower of Baba. One day he asked him, "Shall I accept

Islam?" Baba said to him, "Bring the book." Shri Rao always had the *Geeta* with him. So he placed it in front of Baba.

Baba opened the book and turning its pages he said, "I live in this."

It is said that Shirdi Sai Baba and Baba Tajuddin were heard conversing with each other although they lived at quite a distance from one another.

History has not been able to trace the birth of Shirdi Sai Baba and likewise it has failed to procure the whereabouts of Baba Tajuddin's village.

Krishnadutt

Near Muradnagar Of Ghaziabad District, there is a small village named Khurrampur Salimabad. Here, in 1940, a child was born. When he was forty days old, his mother, shifting him from her own lap, made him lie down straight, in the baby-cot. At that time, the baby started moving his neck now to the right and now to the left and his lips quivered as if he was talking.

On reaching the age when a child actually starts speaking, the moment he would lie down straight, he would start swaying his neck right and left, as usual; one could hear Sanskrit *shlokas* being uttered and pronounced by this child.

As this continued, the people at home thought that he was possessed of some evil spirit, by birth. It was a very poor family. All were illiterate. They grasped neither the sound nor the meaning of the Sanskrit couplets. They began to call the witch-doctors, who would beat the child as well as make him inhale the smoke of various kinds of things.

The child was named Krishnadutt. His childhood was full of miseries. When he grew up a little, he was kept as a servant at the Chaudhrys, to do odd jobs. But this reciting in a trance continued there too. Now people from the neighbouring villages thronged to see this spectacle for curious entertainment. To escape the crowd of these spectators, Krishnadutt left his home and family at the age of fifteen. A Chaudhry family from Barnava saw this boy and took him to their place. Krishnadutt stayed there for almost six years. This recitation and speaking carried on there also. And often it aroused the interest of the people. Krishnadutt went away from there as well. He did not know where to go. This news had reached Delhi, by now. So some people from Delhi made an effort and took him there. The people in the Arya Samaj of Sarojini Nagar saw this and made an attempt to understand this. They realized that it was some mystery of Nature, some energy which was going waste.

Consequently, a Vedic Research committee was formed. Research was conducted on the discourses of Krishnadutt. Whatever he spoke was recorded and then published in the form of a book. Like this, the committee has published fifty five books. They also started a monthly journal called 'Yogic Pravachan.'

Many discourses are replete with secrets and mysteries, what were the sixteen thousand gopies of Krishna? How did Agastya Rishi drink off the ocean? What is Kalpvriksh? What were Gautam and Ahalya? What was the history of Ravan? Once Maharishi Lomash had also spoken in Krishnadutt's voice. One person, Mahanand often spoke in every *pravachan*. It seems from the discourse that Mahanand is some soul which has been wandering as subtle body for millions of years. This soul describes the events of *Dvapar Era* as seen with his own eyes. Also of *Treta-Era* . It appears that in some era, 'Kal' Krishnadutt was a teacher, a guru. That is why that soul asks many questions full of thirsting curiosity.

Krishnadutt could not read or write but when he spoke in a trance, it seemed that it was the voice of a great scholar.

Recently this happening came to an end with the death of Krishnadutt. When he was alive, I had requested the Samiti and had called him over to my place. I saw this amazing spectacle myself. I had also recorded his voice. This scientific mystery of human body has ended with him. It was not explained by any important or exhaustive research. It is not known where the thread of his inner consciousness would connect when he was not really conscious. When he came back to consciousness, that thread got disconnected with memory and recollection. The same voice which would be giving knowledge of the ten dishas, which would be enunciating the essence of the substance of science and scholasticism in the words of some sage, the same voice, when questioned later, about anything, could only say, with much effort — "But I do not know."

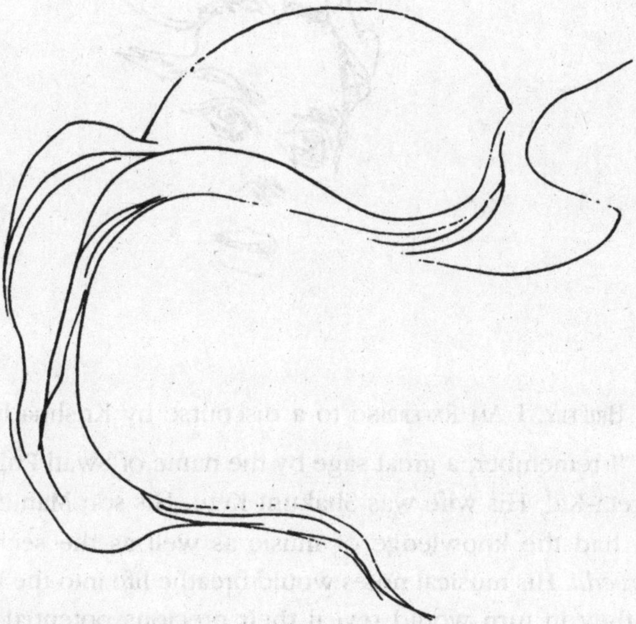

Varun-Ketu

VERY BRIEFLY, I AM REFERRING to a discourse by Krishnadutt ji.

"I remember, a great sage by the name of Swati Pulatsya in Treta-Kal. His wife was Shakunt Ketu. His son Manichand Ketu had the knowledge of music as well as the secret of *Ayurveda.* His musical notes would breathe life into the herbs and they in turn would reveal their precious potentials and qualities to Manichand Ketu.

"Manichand Ketu begot three sons, Varun Ketu, Vibhishan and Suniti Ketu. Varun Ketu was playing in the courtyard one day when Som Bhan, Kriti Bhan, and Ketu Rishi came there. He noticed the forehead of the child. When Pulatsya Rishi and

Manichand Ketu welcomed him and offered him *asan* to sit, he said, 'I have observed Varun Ketu's brow. The child will become a king.'

"The father and son of the family of Rishis were surprised at what the Rishi of *Angis Gotra* had said. The Rishi continued, 'He will definitely become the king but his life, full of splendour, will be cut short.'

"Then the Rishi explained, "There is a certain herb which has to be given to the pregnant mother to drink when the star Swati rules. If it is administered during the effect of any other star, then the intellectual faculty of the child becomes imbalanced." Varun Ketu's father and grandfather found out that this is what had really happened.

When they grew up a little, the three children were sent to Gurukul in order to receive education. It was the *ashram* of Rishi Shukdeshvant. The Rishi saw the foreheads of the three children. He took Pulatsya Rishi aside; when they were alone he told him, "The eldest son Varun Ketu will become a king. But there will be some blemish on his conduct. The second will attain greatness and will finally become a king. The third one will be an eminent scientist."

In this way, in the school of Brahma the three children acquired education and instruction. 'Brahma' is the name given to one who knows the secret of *Vedas*. The word *Brahma* is a title. Shukdeshvant was called Brahma.

Scholastic knowledge was imparted to Varun Ketu. The

practice of rituals and ceremonies was taught to Vibhishan. The instruction of science was given to Suniti Ketu. Varun had a great thirst for the knowledge of the ten directions. Hence the Rishi imparted that —

1. *Agni* (fire) who is full of light, is the god of *Prachidik* (east).

2. *Indra*, the treasure of lightning contained in the clouds, is the god of *Dakshin* (south).

3. *Varun* through whose energy Earth yields food grains, fruits and flowers, is the god of *Pratichidik* (west).

4. *Som* whose *rasa* is known to the *Yogis*, is the god of *Udichi* (north).

One who wanders in Brahma becomes a *brahmachari*. After the churning of knowledge, one who saunters in its glory is known as *Som*. Joining life and mind is *Yoga*.

Starting with the *Mooladhar*, after *Nabhi*, *Hridaya*, *Kantha*, *Swati* and *Trikuti*, comes the *Brahma-randhra*. When *Prana* and *Mana* pass through them and reach the *Brahma-randhra*, there comes a spot called *Pipadsthan* from where atoms spring and flow. The one who drinks it with the tip of his tongue, drinks *Som Rasa*. For him wandering in the universe is easy.

5. *Vishnu*, who preserve and protects, is the god of *Dhrwa* (Earth).

6. *Guru* (Jupiter), the god of knowledge, is the god

of *Urdhva* (sky).

After this are the four angles (*Kon*):

7. *Ishan Kon*, whose god is the *Sun*.
8. *Dakshinay Kon*, whose god is *Aditi*.
9. *Pashchim Kon*, whose god is *Megh*.
10. *Udichi Kon*, whose god is *Ghan*.

Varun Ketu acquired the knowledge of all ten directions. So he came to be called *Dashanan*. The word *'anan'* stands for direction. One who commands the knowledge of ten *dishas* is, therefore, *Dashanan*.

Younger brother Vibhishan attained the knowledge of *Karmakand*. *Karmakand* means the scientific knowledge of each organ and the performance of scientific actions. This human body is a *Yagya-Shala* where the fire of heart is built.

To wander in the waves of knowledge is known as science. To know the elements, Sun, Air, Water and to know their waves and vibrations is what the third brother Suniti learnt and absorbed that knowledge within him. It was exactly as a pitcher contains and absorbs water in it. Hence Suniti ketu is called Kumbh Karan, -'Kumbh' meaning a pitcher.

During the period of learning, Varun Ketu was of a restless temperament. Once he took his guru's daughter to a lonely spot and molested her.

The girl wailed and wept before she died and cursed

him that whenever he would force himself on a woman his head would split into pieces and his dynasty would terminate.

Mahidant, the king of Mahiraj, used to be an emperor at one time. Lanka also was under his rule. But with time Kuber became the Monarch of Lanka and Raja Mahidant was left with a small kingdom. His daughter was Mandodari, who was educated in Rishi Ashram. The news of Mandodari's beauty spread like moonlight all around, while the father was worried and wished to find a right husband for her.

Finally, when he saw Varun Ketu, the elder son of Manichand Ketu, he selected him for his daughter.

At that time Varun Ketu was forty eight years old. A large number of *Rishis* went to Mahidant's kingdom to attend the wedding. Mandodari garlanded Varun Ketu with *Manimala*, a garland made of jewels and gems. Raja Mahidant had only one regret, that Lanka was no longer ruled by him; so he could not give as much to his daughter as he wanted to. Varun Ketu realized why the king was so sad. He raised an army, by asking for ten thousand soldiers each from various kings, to win over Lanka. When Kuber saw the size of army, he surrendered Lanka to Varun Ketu, without fighting a battle. Varun Ketu meant to hand over the kingdom of Lanka to Mahidant but the latter gifted it back to Varun Ketu as a dowry for his daughter's marriage.

"Varun Ketu being from a family of rishis, his father and grandfather felt embarassed because the tradition of the and family was based on knowledge and learning and not on ruling a kingdom. Hence, a conference of rishis was called to decide whether Varun Ketu should accept Lanka.

"The *rishis* pronounced the decision that the kingdom should be accepted and on this occasion the name Ravana was given to Varun Ketu. 'Ravana' means Mahadani, the great giver. When the rishis and kings assembled for the ceremony of coronation, Maharishi Kukut Muni was chosen as the head of the assembly. He stood in the *sabha* and declared, "I shall not perform his *Raj Tilak*. I have seen and studied his fore-brow, he can well acquire the knowledge of the ten directions, but is not capable of becoming a king. One who cannot hold the society in high esteem is not fit to be a king. His stars foretell that he shall be a king. So shall he be! But I shall not perform his *Raj Tilak* with my hands."

The coronation was performed but not by Kukut Muni.

OSHO RELATES TO US, "I was studying in school. I went to my teacher to ask for seven days' leave as I was going away to die."

"The teacher scolded me that it was madness and asked whether I was going to commit suicide."

"I told my teacher of the prediction of an astrologer who had warned me that after every seven years there was maran-yog on me. 'Now I am fourteen years old. The first probable period of my death was when I was seven. But that got averted. This is the second maran-yog. People at home are sorrowful about my imminent death. Well, this time I am going to sit for seven days, intending to be conscious when death comes, so that I am able to feel it.'

"I went away to a temple outside the village. It was a lonely, remote, dilapidated temple. No one ever visited it. I told the pujari that I was going to stay there peacefully for seven days. I requested him to supply me something to eat once a day. Thus, for seven days I kept waiting for my death. These seven days were an extraordinary experience for

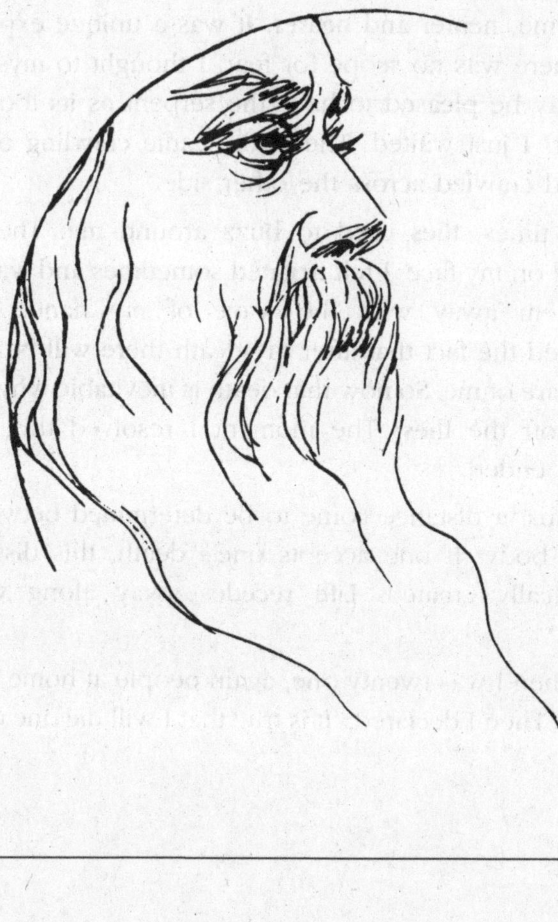

me. Death did not take me but I for one, tried my utmost to die. Many strange things happened but the basic point is that once you are ready to die you become silent and peaceful. You are totally devoid of anxiety. All worries are for life as such. Being alive is the root of all anxieties. If you are prepared for death any day, then where is the worry?

"I was passing my days in the temple. On the third or the fourth day a snake appeared. I kept watching it. I was not at all frightened. Suddenly, I felt that the snake was coming towards me, nearer and nearer. It was a unique experience where there was no scope for fear. I thought to myself that death may be pleased to have the serpent as its tool. Then why fear? I just waited. The snake came crawling over my body and crawled across the other side.

"At times, flies used to buzz around me. They even swarmed on my face. I felt irritated sometimes and wanted to drive them away with the wave of my hand. Then I considered the fact that after my death there will be no one to take care of me. So now that death is inevitable why should I wave off the flies? The moment I resolved this, all my irritation ended.

"Thus, a distance come to be determined between me and my body. If one accepts one's death, this distance is automatically created. Life recedes away along with all worries.

"When I was twenty one, again people at home became worried. Then I declared, 'It is true that I will die one day. But right now I am not going to die. However, the forecast by the astrologer was a great help to me. It made me acquainted with death much in advance. Death was constantly in my mind. I accepted that it had to come one day.

"Death can be used for deep meditation. It is then that the inner energy travels to the inner soul freeing itself from the world. No truth can ever be comprehended by merely thinking. If a flower has bloomed, you can never fully understand it by thinking about it. The more you ponder, the more you will lose the flower. The difference between 'seeing' and 'thinking' is of paramount importance. The West lays stress on 'thinking'. Hence it has given the name, Philosophy, to the science of thinking. Here we call the science of thinking by the name, *Darshan Shastra*. 'Darshan' means to see..."

Osho Katha

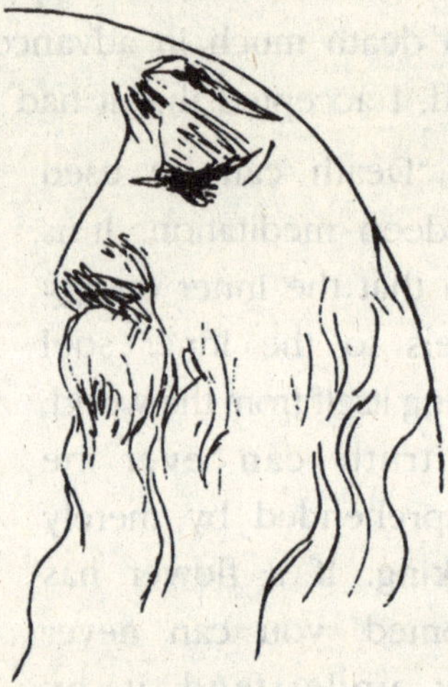

A CERTAIN PERSON RECEIVED *DEEKSHA* from Osho and took *Sanyas*. After seven years suddenly one day he returned to say, "Now that I am free from fear, I can declare that seven years back when I had come to Ahmedabad, I had not come to take sanyas but had come to murder you." Osho smiled and just remarked, "Once again?" That person did not comprehend and continued, "I had a revolver. That day's meeting was attended by so many people that I could not find myself a place to sit, in the hall. So the organizers arranged for me to squat on the stage itself where you were seated."

Osho asked, "Then, why did you let an opportunity like

this slip away?"

This man replied, "Before this, I had never heard your speech. That day when you spoke, I could not but go on listening to you. My mind was transformed. Instead of assassinating you, I accepted your sermons. I took *deeksha.*"

Osho smiled and visualized. A long chain of events flashed upon his mind. He knew that seven hundred years ago, the disciple who had poisoned him and had caused his death was this very man.

Osho stood mute under a tree for a while. Lo! the flowers and foliage of the tree smiled. Perhaps no other preacher-saint had ever before acquired this ultimate honour.

One who came to assassinate him was instead ordained with his preaching. He received *deeksha* and sat at Osho's feet.

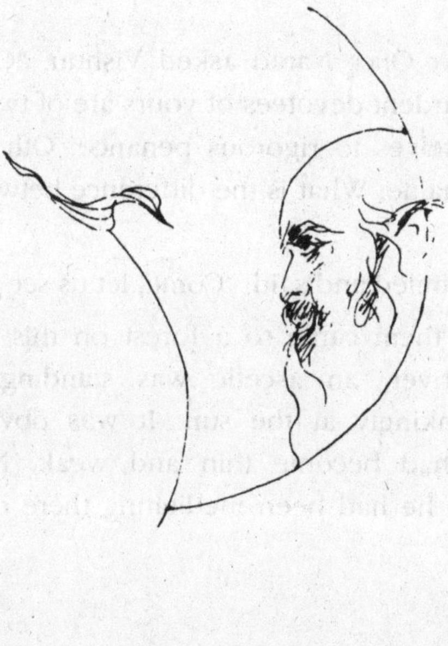

A Scarlet Flower

It Is Said That Once Narad asked Vishnu, "O, Lord of the world, these ardent devotees of yours are of two types. Some subject themselves to rigorous penance. Others dance and sing to your name. What is the difference between these two paths?"

Vishnu smiled and said, "Come, let us see for ourselves."

Both of them came to a forest on this earth. On the bank of a river, an ascetic was standing on one leg gazing unblinkingly at the sun. It was obvious that one of his legs had become thin and weak. No one knew for how long he had been meditating there on one leg. As

Narad and Vishnu went to him, he was grateful that Vishnu himself has blessed him with his *Darshan*. So he asked, "O, my Lord, now that you have come, please tell me how much more penance still remains? When shall I merge in your flame?"

Vishnu answered, "O, hermit, there are only two more births for you."

As he heard this, the dark shadows of the setting sun spread over his face. Extremely distressed, he uttered, "Still two more births?" Simmering with rage, he pressed his lean leg and looked at Vishnu.

Vishnu and Narad smiled and went ahead in the forest. The sound of someone's singing came floating along with the wind. They moved in that direction now. As they approached, they noticed that a man, playing with the boughs of a tree, was fully engrossed in himself and was singing away with deep feeling. He seemed to be conversing with each and every leaf. He was even oblivious of the fact that two persons came and stood next to him. As Vishnu stepped forward and touched him on the shoulder, he was so moved that with moist eyes he saw that Lord Vishnu was standing there in person.

The ascetic was overwhelmed with devotion, touched Vishnu's feet and said, "How very gracious these flowers and leaves have been to me that I am able to actually see my own Lord Vishnu. Now that you have blessed me with your presence, please do tell me when I will merge in your flame."

Vishnu told him that he would have to take as many births as the leaves of that tree.

On hearing this that man went into raptures of dancing. His forehead glowed with the reddish hue of the rising sun and he exclaimed,. “Is that all! These many lives I shall easily pass, just dancing and singing. I thank you, for you have given me such hope, my lord!”

At that moment Narad observed that the seed of love which had been in that man’s heart had blossomed into a scarlet flower. This flower would never wither away.

A Dervesh

Osho Narrates The Story Of a *dervesh* who lived in ancient times. The gods had seen his inner light. So they came themselves, greeted him and said, "Ask for any benediction. You shall be granted what you desire." The *dervesh* said, "There is nothing to ask for. I do not desire anything. It is gracious of you to have come." The gods said, "Now, that we have come we must give something. You just have to say it. What do you want?" The *dervesh* said, "I cannot think of anything. All I can say is that I shall accept what so ever you give me."

The gods said, "We bestow upon you a boon that

whomsoever you touch will be cured no matter how ill he is. So much so, that even if it is a dead body, it will come to life and get up."

The *dervesh* said, "This will create a big problem for me. The corpse shall get up alive but it will be my death. As I go on practising this, I will start feeling that I am the doer. As soon as this ego of 'I' sets in within me, I shall virtually die."

The gods thought it over and said, "Alright, let it be so, that, on who so ever your shadow falls, will get cured of his pain or disease. Under your shade, people will get well."

The *dervesh* requested, "Kindly do this much favour to me. My neck should always remain straight and not be able to turn and look back."

The gods granted, "May it be so!"

It is said that whichever way the *dervesh* passed, the dry trees there would turn green, flowers would bloom. Sick people's distresses and diseases disappeared. The drought hit places would be blessed with rainfall. If any wells had salt water, it would become sweet."

After many years when his end was near and the *dervesh* was about to leave his body, the gods appeared and asked, "Was the benediction bestowed by us effective?"

"I do not know", said the *dervesh*, "I never even glanced back. I wouldn't know what happened. I continued walking straight on my own path!"

Anxious Mother; Grieving Earth

THIS STORY COMES DOWN FROM ancient times. A woman was blessed with a son after much entreaties, invocations and prayers.

People marvelled when they saw the infant's face — wide cheerful forehead, smiling eyes. They also saw that the child's legs were closed in *padmasan*. His mother would straighten his legs when the body slept in his cot. But again they would form the lotus pose.

This news spread all over the town and even to the nearby villages. An eminent astrologer himself came to see the child and declared, "The Sun and the Moon are present in the infant's eyes; sun in the right and moon in the left. The protector of the pupil is the highly placed Saturn. His vision is ruled by a powerful Mars. The big bold eyes indicate that Jupiter, too, is sitting with the sun and the Moon."

The child's mother quietly listened and said, "O, knower of stars, tell me what he will be when he grows up."

The astrologer stated that he would be a great philanthropist of such renown that his fame would spread like fragrance in all directions. His speech would be the voice of God.

The astrologer had hardly uttered as much when the eyes of the child's mother brimmed with tears. She said, "Then tell me this, O, learned one! When will my son be assassinated?"

The astrologer was taken aback at the nature of question. Mother's eyes filled with tears every now and again. She picked up the child, pressed it to her bosom and said, "I had begged and prayed to be blessed with a son endowed with a long life!" Soon she controlled herself and asked further, "O, Priest! tell me at least this much. Will his murder take place before his death or after?" The astrologer was even more perplexed with this unusual question. The woman continued, "If God speaks through his voice, then all those who carry out business in the name of God, those sitting in shops set up in the name of God, will become his enemies. They will find modes to murder him."

The shocked astrologer told her, "Devi, he will not be any body's enemy. His speech will be a voice full of love."

"That is exactly what I am saying", said the woman wiping her eyes with the corner of her veil.

"If he speaks the language of love, then how will people slay each other? All those who create martyrs in the name of religion will be highly disturbed. Their business will not flourish. They, therefore, will get him assassinated first and foremost."

The astrologer could only stare at her face silently. So she said, "If this does not happen, then great monuments will be built after his name, when his life ends. The caretakers of these places, sitting there to misappropriate the donations and offerings, will engage themselves in numerous controversies and arguments. Many new places of worship will be erected and many will first be demolished. In that case, it will be the death of the inner light which he had spread.

The soul that will voice his words will be slain. That indeed will be his own assassination. Won't it be?"

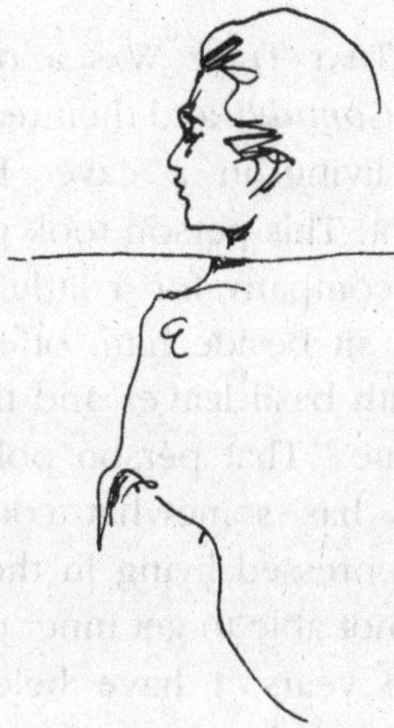

Lamp of the Brow

THEY SAY THAT THERE WAS a person who went to *Ganga, Gangotri, Gomukh* and then reached *Tapovan*. There he saw a *Sadhu* living in a cave His brow was tranquil and resplendent. This person took permission from the hermit to be in his company for a little while. The man of the cave made him sit beside him, offered him tea which he made himself with basil leaves and then asked, "Well, good man, now tell me." That person politely said, "The water of the mountains has somewhat cooled down my heart which became depressed living in the cities. Yet, I want to know why I am not able to get inner peace? I have studied *Shastras* for twelve years. I have held discourses with renowned scholars. But the apparent outcome was only their arrogance and my mind's restlessness.

The hermit of the cave smiled and said, "I shall relate a story to you. Once someone was caught on the charge of murder. When he was in the lockup, the other criminals asked him, 'We heard that you have killed somebody. Whom did you kill? Did you avenge an old enmity?'

"That man replied, 'I have no enemy. Nor have I fed a grudge. Nor have I murdered anyone. I found an already committed murder.'

"The fellow-prisoners laughed. This man went on to say, 'I went to the fields early in the morning at the break of dawn. Someone had been murdered, whose body was lying there. The police has forcefully caught hold of me and has brought me here."

The *sadhu* of the cave narrated and laughed. He said, "Even if an already committed murder is blamed on someone; even if his punishment is pronounced; yet, he knows in the heart of his hearts that he is innocent. But these learned men of ours, who find the already expounded *Shastras* fail to understand that they themselves have done nothing.

"Look, you good man, if the murder already committed does not make you a sinner in inner-mind, then how can holy virtues be attributed to one by the readymade knowledge of others?

"The lamp of the brow has to burn with the oil of one's own experience."

Politics and Dharma

I WISH TO RELATE To you an incident which has taken the form of a tradition that is prevalent even today. To this date in a village called Samvatsar in Maharashtra, in the month of *Chaitra*, a delightful festival is celebrated every year. This village is situated on both banks of river Godavari. The name of the village on one bank is Samvatsar Khurd and the one on the bank across is Samvatsar Budara.

In the month of *Chaitra* when the river dries up, people gather together on both banks. They beat drums and clang small cymbals and the woman from both sides participate in a tug-of-war while the menfolk of both banks throw stones at each other. The daughter of the chieftain of the village, which wins in the tug-of-war, is taken away by the victorious villagers and then that abducted girl is worshipped. They apply vermillion on her forehead, perform *aarti* for her and the women of the village sing auspicious songs.

Later, a bullock-cart is decorated. The girl is all dressed up with golden and silver tassels and is given a farewell with saris, blouses and numerous gifts. Women sing farewell songs.

"The favourite daughter of our land is returning after a long journey."

Thus, the girl who was forcefully taken away is sent back very honourably.

The other party extends welcome to those abductors who come to return this girl. They offer a feast of *puris* and curry as a mark of welcome.

A historical event which took place in Shivaji's time is the background of this tradition. During a battle, one of Shivaji's *subedars* got the daughter-in-law of a Muslim *Subedar* of Kalyan abducted. Shivaji learnt about it and the girl was brought to his court. Shivaji gave her many expensive gifts and he arranged that she is returned with much respect.

They say that certain ministers in the court questioned Shivaji, "Your Majesty, what sort of politics is this?"

Shivaji's reply was, "This is the *dharma* of politics; no politics is devoid of *dharma*."

What is politics? What is *dharma?* What is loyalty? What is law? To preserve and register all this in the memory of the people, this tradition came to be practised. In the village Samvatsar, therefore, it is celebrated with immense enthusiasm till today.

Politics, Dharma and Law

THERE USED TO BE A person who was ever thirsting for spiritual knowledge. He observed that in the name of LIFE as led by people and the way they live is not really a LIFE in the true sense. Some people lived under tremendous oppression whose dreams were snatched away from their eyes.

He thought to himself. What is law? What is justice? What is this whole system? He could not find an answer anywhere. So he went to a *rishi* and put this question to him. The *rishi* said to him, "Listen, I shall relate an incident. It happened in the times when after the death of the father, the son used to offer things as sacrifice for the soul of the dead father. The hand of the father, who had reached the subtle body, used to actually extend and accept the sacrifice. During those days, a certain king died. His son took some fruits and flowers in his hand and wished to make an offering to his father. First one hand appeared before him, then came the second and then the third. The prince was confused. Did I have three fathers?

This question was acute.

No one was able to answer it. It was learnt that in a state nearby which was now under the authority of this state, there lived a learned scholar who was capable of answering a question like this. The prince went to him. He was told, "Look, son, I cannot give you an answer to this. But there is a river around here. Far away, somewhere on its bank, a woman lives in a small hut. She seems to be somewhat out of her mind. But I am certain that she will be able to answer your question." The prince searched and found that hut and posed this question to that woman. It was about evening time. The woman lighted a lamp in the hut. Then she groped for the prince's arm and asked, "Is a diamond tied around your arm from the time of your birth?" The prince was amazed. He said, "Yes, mother. The diamond is really tied around my arm. They say that it has been there ever since my birth." The woman who seemed a little out of her mind said, "Look son, I shall answer your question. But you will have to promise that you will offer the *Pitr-dan* to that one who is suggested by me. As the prince assured her of this, the woman kissed his forehead and went on to say, "The king of this state was a very noble man. When he passed away, his officers conspired and in order to take possession of the state, they imprisoned the young prince. They were about to kill him. Before killing anyone, it is customary to ask what the person's last wish is. When this was asked, he replied, that , he wished to get married before he died. This was his last wish. It had to be fulfilled. So the message was sent around the city that the parents who would give their young and beautiful daughter in marriage to this prince who was about to die, would be given substantive wealthier return. The woman embraced the prince and admitted, "I am that girl, who married that dying prince. My parents were very poor. I knew that they would never be able to get me married. Therefore I accepted this condition. I was wedded to the prince. We had just one night to meet and live. It was now, that the officers realized their mistake, that it was the prince's foresight. He had really been very foresighted. He wanted to leave his seed in her womb before his death. They realized that when his son would grow up he could take over the state. The officers, therefore, warned, 'We have fulfilled the last wish of the person who is about to die. But he will not be allowed to touch his wife. That was not included in the wish.' So the prince was allowed some time to talk to his wife. There was guard on all four sides."

"The woman further narrated, 'Son, during that allotted time my husband, the prince, gave me a diamond so that I could sell it and live my life comfortably. Then he gave me a second diamond and also ordered me that I should buy a seed from a handsome, young man, in exchange of this diamond. Then he gave me a third diamond so that I would tie it round the arm of my son when he was born. This diamond, he said, would protect my son, always. This was all. The meeting was over. Next day the prince was killed.

'Then, my son, I acted as I was told by my husband. I sold one diamond and got a small palace built where I began to stay. Then I searched for a man and purchased his seed in exchange of the second diamond. But when I conceived you, that man went back on his word. He wanted to live with me forcefully. He did not want to leave. Hence I left everything, started staying in a forest secretly. Then you were born but I knew that my enemies were on the prowl to search me out. Therefore I tied the third diamond round your arm and placed you in a small basket of flowers and let it float down the river. I knew that the diamond would protect you. That is exactly what has happened. When the king of the adjoining state came to bathe in the river, he saw the flower basket, saw you and picked you up. The king had no child. So he took you to the astrologer and asked them whether the child would be strong and powerful when he grew up.

"The king was getting old. He wanted that some strong person should stay with him who could expand his kingdom. He wanted that the neighbouring states should also come under his rule.

That seemingly distraught mother said, "Look son, one

who sold his seed, is your father. The one who brought you up to enhance his strength with a motive is your father. But your real father is he who resolved you solemnly within his soul and within himself."

And while relating this incident, the rishi said, "O, curious one! eager for knowledge! Now you know. The law whose ingredient is purchased is not true law. Moreover, the law, which is formulated to amplify the power and force of someone is not real law either. Pure law is the one which carries within itself the resolution of justice."

The *Rishi* smiled. He said, "That alone is law, that alone is politics, in whose inner soul, *Dharma*, exists."

Pegs and Ropes

Once There Was An Inn in a certain desert. A caravan of camels halted there for a night. The travellers fixed pegs and tied their camels with ropes. They noticed that they were short of one peg and one rope. This got them worried that one camel would remain untied and might lost at night in the desert. They went to request the inn-keeper, "Brother, if you have a spare peg and rope, please, lend us for the night. Tomorrow morning when we leave, we shall return them to you."

The inn-keeper suggested, "I do not have either peg or rope. But if you listen to me, I can offer you a solution. Your camel will sleep peacefully at night. In the morning include him in your caravan and take him along." This device, however, was extremely unique. He continued, "You dig and fix a peg which is not there. Then you tie a rope, which again is not there, around the camel's neck. Then you pat him and ask him to sit down. He will just sit through the night."

The people of the caravan were rather astonished. But there was no other way out. With a hammer, they fixed a peg which wasn't there. Then they moved their arms around the camel's neck and tied the rope which wasn't there at all. Now, the camel quietly sat down on the ground.

In the morning the travellers had their tea and drinks in the inn and were all set for the next camp.

They removed all the pegs, coiled up the ropes and put them in bags. All the other camels stood up ready to move further. But that one continued sitting as it was. They tried their best to make him get up but in vain. The camel just refused to rise from the ground.

The people of the caravan were perplexed and wondered whether the man of the inn had cast a spell on the camel and had hypnotised it.

They again went to the inner-keeper to convey that their camel refused to budge. The keeper started laughing. He suggested, "First remove the peg that you had stuck to the ground. Then open the rope tied around the camel's neck. This done, the camel will rise on his own."

These people did as they were told. With the help of the

hammer, they shook and pulled the peg, which was not there. Then they moved their arms round the camel's neck and untied the rope which again was not there. Now, the camel stood up and joined the caravan.

The chief of the caravan took the inn-keeper aside and asked him, "Brother where did you learn this trick?"

The keeper laughed, "I learnt it by observing human beings. Don't you see that all humans in this, our world, are bound by pegs and ropes that do not exist? They are forever bound and they remain in servile obedience to these pegs and ropes that do not exist."

These Fifty Tales

IT IS THE SOIL OF this land that penetrated the mystery of Mahachetna, the Supreme Consciousness. It has experienced the energy flowing into ripples from the originating point. These firm believers, who maintain that God has ordained our births have themselves given birth to God from their own inner-self.

The soil of this land was incessantly soaked in blood.

It was plunged incessantly in ravages and massacres. Even then the lamps of meditation continued to burn in the dark nights. Even as the yokes of slavery clutched or released our neck, the process of deep thinking carried on, it carried on.......

That besides the independence from physical slavery, we had to free ourselves from mental slavery too. We had to liberate ourselves from psychic slavery too. The tales in our history are laden with inner-thinking. Of them, I am relating only fifty today, because our land has completed fifty years of its independence.

I shall not narrate any story for the next year or the years to come.

that all of us ought to pray and write parables of aman or peace.

I know not when it will be! All I can say is, that if ever the rule of PEACE is established in this world, it will sprout here, in Bharat.

Every single particle of this land, even when steeped in tears, contains the essence of Mahachetna, the Supreme Consciousness.

—Amrita